MUD CREEK

KELLY FERGUSON

Fair Park Publishing

CONTENTS

ACKNOWLEDGMENTS

I would like to thank my beautiful wife, Sandi and my friend, Mark Ramano for their kind support.

INTRODUCTION

Mud Creek is a fictional story set in rural Mississippi in 1954. It embodies the powerful struggles which make up the fabric of life: tragedy; chaos; struggle; greed; and overcoming.

Enjoy.

Fair Park Publishing LLC
210 E Main
Tupelo MS 38804
www.fairparkpublishing.com

FAIR PARK PUBLISHING FIRST PUBLISHED WORKS

Library of Congress Cataloging in publication date is available

Photography by Sandra Ferguson 2019 permission granted 2019
Book Design by Jeff Senter
Copy Edited by Bruce A. Brown

This Book was manufactured in the UNITED STATES OF AMERICA
ISBN# 978-1-7341222-0-6 (Hardcopy)
ISBN# 978-1-7341222-1-3 (Paperback)
ISBN# 978-1-7341222-4-4 (E-books)

Nature admits no lie.

— THOMAS CARLYLE

TRAGEDY ON MUD CREEK

Folks didn't call it Mud Creek for nothing. When God mixed water and that lime dirt, it was a great equalizer of men. Mud stuck to you whether you were the great John Watson with 3000 acres or a broke sharecropper with no flour or hope of paying off last year's crop. Folks died within a stone's throw of their birth spot -- few escaped.

Sour mud mixed with the exhaust fumes from Mr. John's new Super M Farmall tractor. Eerie shadows flickered across the water to the drone of the powerful engine. Mr. John shouted to Bully over bull frogs exalting and fat black women cursing the rain.

"Ride that left brake, Bully! Ride that left brake! Don't you dump this load of cotton, boy!"

Mr. John knew Bully outperformed the best farm equipment operators in the county. He gave him hell, just the same. Bully fought the slipping, sliding tractor. Mr. John stood on the wooden "tongue" between the tractor and the old mule wagon. The roughhewn oak tongue was jerry rigged to the new tractor.

Huddled in the mule wagon were squalling kids of every size and description, three barking cur dogs, and seven stoic farm women. All rescued from the cotton fields by Mr. John and Bully moments before the storm hit. Water dripped off their chins, down their elbows, and no dry thread remained. Crack! Boom! Again, and again. Lightning bolts cracked and streaked across the foreboding sky. Children held their ears. Women pulled their babies to their breast.

"Bet this washes the Bonner Bridge out, Mr. John!"

Bully grinned. He backed off the throttle. Bully loved to please Mr. John, which was no easy task. Yet, the two were inseparable. A young woman had conceived Bully. No one ever knew who raped her. Mr. John and his reluctant wife, Lillian, took the two in and provided for them. Mr. John fathered Bully. In the year of nineteen hundred and fifty-four, Mr. John was a giant of a man in Lee County, Mississippi. Clean shaven with a straight back, his six-foot, four inch frame was an imposing figure. He owned three thousand acres of land, a thousand head of cattle, mules and hogs, a cotton gin, and a general store. Bully lived in his father's shadow-- always.

"Both brakes, Bully! Both brakes, son!" Mr. John screamed. Bully fought through the driving rain to keep control of the Farmall. They entered the sharp, slippery, rutted decline toward the fjord at Mud Creek; the giant wheels slid, pushing gray, slimy mud forward.

Without warning, the red iron mule lurched to the left when Bully's rain soaked boot slipped off the right brake. The mule wagon jack knifed, throwing the wooden oak tongue into the giant wheel. CRACK! The smooth tapered wooden tongue exploded in a burst of large splinters and sharp, jagged edges.

Bully fought the wet steering wheel. The Farmall slid

sideways down the steep, slippery grade. The mule wagon, now free, slid parallel with its once master. "Ugh!" Bully fought to stay focused, trying to regain control of the tractor. The mule wagon crashed into the Farmall. Rain whipped sideways. Mr. John screamed. The smell of sour mud, the roaring motor and shrills from the mule wagon's occupants flooded Bully's mind. The mass of new machinery, aged wagon and humanity landed in the bottom of the fjord. There, the swollen waters of Mud Creek greeted them. The momentum of the Farmall carried them out into the swift, rising waters of Mud Creek. It came to rest pointing downstream into the darkness. The mule wagon was lodged between the giant rear wheel and the engine of the Farmall. Bully struggled to find neutral on the H pattern of the transmission. Blood and muddy water battled for crimson control over his soaked leather boots.

The mule wagon had become a death wagon.

Bully looked over the rear tire and his eyes met those of Mr. John's. A moment elapsed where there was no separation--total communication. The steel blue eyes, which Bully both loved and feared, seared. Mr. John grasped the sharp bloody end of the shattered tongue; it protruded from his stomach. Blood flowed from his mouth and ran into the water.

"Bully get the chain off the cotton scale and chain the wagon to the tractor tire!" he said. Blood ran down his chin.

"Oh, god! I'm sorry, Mr. John!" Bully cried.

He clamored off the tractor into waist deep water.

Bully made his way to the wagon where the drenched mass of barking dogs, hysterical women, children, and wet cotton hung to the tractor tire.

"Where's the chain?! Where's the goddamn chain?!" Bully dug through wet cotton, water jugs, shoes, and leftover soaked lunch bags.

"I think it's in the back," a young Negro girl said, her bottom lip quivering.

Bully waded deeper into the current, holding onto iron brackets and crossmembers of the side planks. He climbed the back tailgate. The wagon shifted, releasing the front wheel from the clutches of the Farmall. Bully slipped but regained his grasp. The dark waters of Mud Creek raged. He rammed his hand, arm deep, into the wet cotton. Again. Again. There it was! Under the wet cotton, Bully felt the notched pea scale and the weights. He ran his hands up toward zero pounds and felt the hook. No chain! Damn! Damn! Damn! Pulling back a huge wet mass of cotton, Bully felt the iron chain: rat a tat-tat-tat; steel on wood. Bully fought the current with the burden and hope of the chain back to Mr. John.

"Quick, Bully. You lose the wagon; you lose the women and kids." Mr. John spit blood and mud. Bully ran the chain through the Farmall's cast iron wheel and the wooden spokes of the wagon and hooked the two together. Once again, the mule wagon and the iron beast were wed.

"Bully get those young'uns and women out of the wagon, and send Jessie to get Doc Grasson," Mr. John ordered.

"Everybody git outta that wagon, and Jessie, you run and get Doc Grasson," Bully yelled to his twelve-year-old son.

Women and children clamored from the wagon. Eyes bulged. Faces turned. The women tried to shield the children from the gruesome sight, with little success.

"Oh, my!" cried Betty Mae, one of the older black women who had worked for Mr. John most of her life.

"Jessie! Git! Go!" Bully shouted.

Jessie jumped from the wagon and splashed through the mud and water, running. He faded into the Mississippi night.

Mr. John languished. His body battled the insult; wagon tongue turned lance.

"Betty Mae, get these kids to sing my song while we wait for Doc Grasson," Mr. John whispered. He stared into the dark waters. Willow trees and shadows danced.

Betty Mae lived a devoted life; first to God and then to Mr. John. She sang often for Mr. John. Betty Mae brought the women and children together with a piercing look. Her gaze sent fear into the hearts of the strongest field hand.

"Just a closer walk to thee. My sweet Lord, let it be." Betty Mae whispered the old spiritual. Her bottom lip quivered. Rain washed tears from her face.

Others joined. Sounds melded: the rain, the wild currents of Mud Creek, bullfrogs exalting, the howling wind, the drone of the idling iron mule's engine, and the slow cadence of the drenched choir. They huddled around Mr. John. He lost consciousness somewhere between the second verse and Jessie crawling under the last cattle gap to Doc Grasson's.

———

Miss Lillian raged through the house, banging doors and yelling. Alice Fae, her head bowed, continued her ironing in the corner of the kitchen. Miss Lillian's posture was ramrod straight. Her words escaped through clinched teeth. She possessed no tolerance for tardiness, Mr. John's included. She hated storms.

"They should be here by now! Damn it! I told John to come outta the fields early if it stormed!" Miss Lillian ranted. She ran her hand through her gray, short cropped hair.

"Pickup that dress, Alice Fae! I swear, girl!" She snarled. "You are nothing but white trash! I don't know why I put up with you!" Miss Lillian barked, wringing her hands in her apron.

Mr. John, well known throughout the county, out matched Miss Lillian only by a bit--she had her ways. She once walked into Judge Claxton's courtroom and chastised him for having a cow running loose. She was fearless.

Alice Fae first met Miss Lillian when Bully brought her home, disclosed her pregnancy and announced their marriage date. Alice Fae's parents consented; she was twelve at the time. Bully had just turned thirteen. Alice Fae exuded frail-ness, but *shy* failed to describe her. She made little eye contact, hid behind thin dark hair that covered her face, and never spoke unless spoken to. Every day, the men and women left for the fields and Alice Fae walked toward Miss Lillian's and Mr. John's house. No one offered to trade places with her.

———

Jessie ran even after cutting his foot while rolling under the first cattle gap. He made excellent time toward Doc Gras-son's. He knew shortcuts. Doc Grasson's farmhouse appeared through the torrential rain. Its fresh coat of white paint glis-tened under the glow of the porchlight. No one knew the age of the old country doctor. He wasn't about to tell anyone, either. However, his full mane of silver-gray hair struck his shoulders and his slight limp gave the country folks a clue. He delivered most of the babies, set most of the broken bones and pulled the sheet over most of the dead between Euclatubba and Jug Fork.

"Doc Grasson! Doc Grasson!" Jessie said. He pounded on the screen.

The hall light came on during Jessie's commotion. He

could see Doc Grasson making his way to the door in his red plaid pajamas.

"Come quick! Mr. John's been stabbed by a big stick, and he's all bloody and everything!" Jessie explained, dripping water and mud on the gray floor of the wooden porch.

Doc Grasson slipped on a pair of overalls and boots and grabbed his black bag. They left the sanctuary of the house and ran for his green 1951 Chevy pickup.

"Jessie, tell me exactly what happened," Doc Grasson questioned climbing into the truck.

"It's bad, Doc," Jessie explained.

Doc Grasson pumped the accelerator with his left foot and hit the floor starter with his right foot. The engine came to life. Jessie continued, "Me and all these dogs and Betty Mae and these women were in the wagon. Daddy and Mr. John were pulling us through the mud and rain and stuff. We started sliding and going sideways and everything and..."

"Slow down, child. Where is the wagon and Mr. John?"

"Mud Creek fjord," Jessie blurted out. "Then the thing between the wagon and the tractor broke and stabbed Mr. John in the stomach, and he's all bloody and everything!" Jessie rambled.

Doc Grasson made his way over the muddy roads and through the driving rain.

Rain poured in sheets. The wind swirled around the truck, trying to dislodge Doc Grasson's Chevy from the gravel road. They made their way toward the Mud Creek fjord. The vacuum powered windshield wipers created a rhythmic sound. They struggled to displace the torrential rain. Doc Grasson, always the clinician, noticed Jessie rocking back and forth in cadence with the windshield wipers. He chanted an audible singsong. Doc Grasson knew extreme stress symptoms when he saw them. Turning a long

sweeping curve in the muddy road, they could see the tractor's lights in the distance through the rain, mist and gloomy
darkness.

Betty Mae saw Doc Grasson's truck lights first. She held
Mr. John's hand and refused to let go. The words of the old
spiritual cracked through her pressed lips. Bully paced back
and forth, muttering to himself and periodically bashing his
head on the mule wagon. The women ignored him and
attended to Mr. John. Bully, too, saw the lights and slogged
through the mud toward the truck. Doc stopped on the firm
surface of the road.

"It's bad, Doc! It's real bad!" Bully screamed, wild eyed.

The rain pounded his face.

"Get me to him, Bully," Doc Grasson directed, holding his
hat and bag.

Bully led with Doc in close pursuit. Jessie jumped out of
the truck and followed the two men, who moved at a very
rapid pace along the water filled, rutted road. When the three
arrived, the huddle of field hands parted, and Doc Grasson
rushed to Mr. John's side, where death welcomed the old
country doctor. Death and Doc Grasso knew one another
well. Doc Grasson reached across Betty Mae's hand and
directed his light on to Mr. John's expressionless face. He
lifted an eyelid and closed it, then he pressed the wrist
attached to the hand Betty Mae held. Bully, Jessie, Betty Mae,
the other field hands and children waited for Doc Grasson to
tell them what they already knew.

"Mr. John has passed on," Doc Grasson whispered. He
removed Mr. John's hand from Betty Mae's clinging grasp.

He spoke into Betty Mae's ear in a kind, but firm voice.
"Betty Mae, you and the women folk take the children to my
truck. They have seen too much."

Betty Mae barked without hesitation, "Git in that truck,

now!" She met no resistance. Doc Grasson turned to Bully, who had become a man of prayer, sitting atop the Farmall.

"You can pray later, Bully. Help me get Mr. John off this damn death contraption!"

Rain poured off Doc Grasson's hat brim.

"Whose idea was this? You got one foot in the nineteenth century and one foot in the twentieth century!"

"It was an accident, Doc, I swear," Bully pleaded, climbing off the tractor.

"We can sort all that out later, Bully. Grab his left hand, and when I count to three, pull! One, two, three pull! Pull! Pull!"

Bully's grasp slipped, and he fell back into the creek and current. He grabbed the wheel of the tractor.

"God dammit, Bully! Get back up here before I die of pneumonia!" Doc said.

Bully struggled to regain his footing in the moving water and pulled himself back to his position.

"I don't know if I can do this, Doc."

"You damn well can. Now, 1, 2, 3 pull! Pull!"

Mr. John's body moved. and the shattered tongue retracting from sight through his bloody shirt.

"Again. Pull!"

Mr. John's body came off the broken tongue; both men struggled under his considerable weight.

"Don't let him go, Bully!" Doc commanded. "Work him around to the side of the wagon."

Both men fought the current and the down pour. Pushing; pulling. They extracted Mr. John from the muddy water.

"Don't stop, Bully. We're moving, let's go!"

The two men gained speed. They drug the limp body through the mud to the awaiting truck and collapsed on all fours, gasping for breath.

"This was not in my Hippocratic oath," Doc muttered to himself.

Children smashed their faces against the three back windows of the Chevy.

The field hands helped Bully place Mr. John in the back of Doc Grasson's Chevy. Bully drove the Farmall back to the equipment shed. Doc Grasson drove the children and the field hands out of the bottom, down Ginny Ridge, over the nearest bridge crossing Mud Creek, and on to Mr. John's place. Miss Lillian didn't handle Doc Grasson's news well. She threatened to kill Bully. She slapped and bit Alice Fae in the face. She was restrained by the field hands. Doc Grasson gave her a strong sedative and called her sister, who stayed the night with the despondent woman.

THE FUNERAL

There is something about a southern funeral. The telephone party lines buzzed for four straight days up and down the ridge.

What was going to happen to Miss Lillian?

How awful that Miss Francina was at that highfalutin' music school in Europe.

Was she going to miss her father's funeral? Had anyone seen Bully?

Was he and Mr. John drinking that night?

Whose idea was it to hitch a tractor to that mule wagon?

Was this God's way of saying Mr. John got too big in the farming business?

Was this Mr. John's punishment for taking in that bastard child, Bully?

The Reverend John Strawrack preached Mr. John's funeral. His mighty frame lost only to his booming voice. He stood six foot, six inches and weighed two hundred and fifty-five pounds. The deep lines in his face and his full shock of grey hair reflected his age. A huge wart affixed itself to his right cheek. The children gawked at the reverend's wart and

his mangled right hand; a victim of a mule drawn mower accident. His middle three fingers were missing, leaving only his
thumb and little finger. When "caught up in the Holy Spirit,"
he waved that hand around and beat on his frayed Bible. On
occasion, his mangled hand hit that wart, which caused
massive bleeding. His voice resonated across the hills when
possessed with the Spirit. Children fought for a front row
seat; any ploy to get a close look at his mangled hand and his
bleeding wart.

People packed Mt. Zion church that Saturday afternoon.
Mt. Zion was a beautiful, yet simple small church hidden
back in the woods. The church men kept the grounds neat,
and it always had a fresh coat of white paint. Old timers told
how Confederate troops used it for a hospital during the
Battle of Brice's Cross Roads. A cemetery behind the church
flourished with stately dogwood trees. People drove for miles
to see the fragrant white blossoms each spring.

Word got out folks drove all the way from Memphis for
Mr. John's funeral.

Women folk banded together and brought enough food to
feed Christian and heathens alike. Baked chicken, BBQ, fried
chicken, cornbread dressing, black eyed peas, mashed pota-
toes, pickled peaches, fried okra and every cake imaginable.
The whole community planned on feasting at Miss Lillian's
after the funeral.

The parishioners buzzed with concern over the where
abouts of Bully. Rumors flew: *had he gone and killed himself? Was
he drunk in the hills? Had he gone off to be by himself and suffered an
accident?* Alice Fae and Jessie worried. Bully exuded depend-
ability and punctuality in family matters. Mr. John had
stressed these qualities to Bully.

The heat radiated off the ground creating distorted
images of the azaleas and irises planted in neat rows near the

church, reminiscent of the dreaded afternoons of July. Church windows were flung open. Folks, in their Sunday best, trying to stay cool, used funeral home fans and last Sunday's bulletins to fan themselves. Miss Tillman, sweat dripping, was positioned at the piano where generations of members passed through the small church. No one could remember how long she'd been there, and the unspoken rule was, don't ask. Doc Grasson took his usual seat over by Miss Tillman. Jessie and Alice Fae, a small bandage over her right eye, was behind Doc Grasson. Alice Fae guarded a space for Bully, though people were standing along the walls.

A hush fell over the congregation when Miss Lillian, dressed in black and looking gaunt, entered with her sister. Reverend Strawrack met the widow, placing his huge arm around her and offered his condolences. She made her way to the front row where Mr. John lay in a simple open casket. Most people said he made a mighty handsome corpse. Miss Lillian maintained her ridged posture throughout the ordeal until she saw Mr. John's ashen face. She crumbled at the sight. Mr. John was dressed in his favorite suit; he wore his gold 32-degree Mason pin on his lapel. The minister and her sister, Beatrice, assisted Miss Lillian to her seat The Reverend Strawrack nodded to Miss Tillman. She opened the hymn book and began to play, "Just a Closer Walk with Thee."

Everyone in the congregation eyed the widow and the door. Tension rose by the minute. *Where was Bully? How could he not attend Mr. John's funeral? He idolized Mr. John.*

"We have come here today to bury Mr. John Watson!" Rev. Strawrack boomed across the congregation. "Who was this man, John Watson? There are those of you who might say he was a good father! There are those of you who might say he was a kind man!"

"Amen!" shouted Mr. Percy.

Mr. Flavous Percy, the oldest member of the church, led the Amen corner. The Amen corner was comprised of an esteemed group of old men who were past giving a damn what people thought. They provided the minister with much needed feedback while he preached.

"There are those of you who might say he was a gentleman." Rev. Strawrack's voice fell like a hog on a frozen pond. "I'll tell you who John Watson was! John Watson was a sinner in the eyes of the Lord!" Rev. Strawrack's voice resonated off the back of the church.

"All of you are sinners in the eyes of the Lord!"

"Amen, that's good preaching!" shouted Mr. Percy, which was like turning a pit bull loose in a chicken house.

The Reverend Strawrack rocked back and forth. His eyes rolled. His rising and falling cadence seduced the congregation into a synchronization just short of mesmerizing. Sweat and spit flew. The minister's mangled right hand flailed. His wart bled. His left hand clutched his Bible.

"In ISAIAH, Chapter 33, verse 10-12, the Bible says, 'Now I will arise, says the LORD, now I will lift myself up; now I will be exalted. You conceive of chaff; you bring forth stubble; your breath is a fire that will consume you. And the people will be as if burned to lime, like thorns cut down, that are burned in the fire." The minister railed with veins protruding from his neck, reminiscent of muscadine vines trying to strangle a water oak tree.

"Amen, that's good preaching!" shouted Mr. Percy during a brief lull in the pious storm.

"And you, young ladies," the Reverend said, pointing to two young pubescent girls on the front row. "Cross your legs and close the gates of Hell! Yes, you too are sinners in the eyes of the Lord." The two young girls started to cry; their mothers led them out with tissues in abundance.

This was more like a mugging than a funeral. He took every advantage; the large congregation braced for his righteous licks.

Reverend Strawrack pounded the altar.

The eyes of the congregation grew wide. A collective gasp erupted from the audience. Bully entered the sanctuary through a door behind the pulpit.

It's hard to say what makes a man do what he does. There are certain checks and balances that hold behaviors and actions within a limited number of predictable responses. Then there is a shift, a disturbance in the balance, which calls all bets off, and a new order emerges that is both unknown and sometimes terrifying.

This was one of those moments.

Bully stuck a double-barreled shotgun to the back of the minister's head. "Shut up and sit down!"

The congregation froze. Miss Lillian fainted with a thud. Bully's eyes, glazed over from huge amounts of alcohol and nights with no sleep, glared. He wore the same pair of overalls he wore the night of the accident. Lime mud was caked in his hair and around his legs, and his boots were long gone. His voice trembled, and his hands shook. He held the cocked shotgun with a glare; he knew no friend. The reverend cowed in the preacher's chair. Alice Fae cringed. She sunk down in the pew clutching Jessie.

"That's my daddy, Mamma! I want my daddy!"

Alice Fae pulled Jessie toward her. "Hush, child! Stay with your mamma."

"None of you knew Mr. John! I'm the only one who knew this man! Not even you, Miss Lillian!" Bully's voice resonated strong and burned with emotion.

"We worked together! We rode home from the fields every night together! You were asleep! We figured out how to fix things, make things, do things. We coon hunted together."

Bully turned to the quaking man of God. "Do not *ever* let me hear you say you knew John Watson. I'll shoot you like a dog! You did not know John Watson. He took me in when the rest of you would have run me and my momma outta town! For years, you made me feel like an outsider. I always tried to be a part of this place. Would you let me in? No! Hell, no!"

Frustration and hurt poured from Bully.

"I jumped your goddamn cars off! I helped you get your goddamn cows back home!" Tears streamed down his face. "I stopped and helped you fix your goddamn flat tires! Mr. John, you always told me to give them time," Bully cried. He stared at Mr. John's corpse. "Well, to hell with'um, Mr. John; times up!"

The first shot took out the new chandelier, which hung in the center of the small church. It crashed into the center aisle. The second shot meant for the piano missed and hit the baptism. Water cascaded through the church. Bully threw the shotgun. It hit a stained-glass window glass and chaos exploded. Bully left the way he came.

C.C. BATES MEETS KILLER

Folks were in a talking frenzy down at the store the following Monday morning. The whole county read about the funeral incident in the *Gazette*. Rumors and questions flew. *Some said Sheriff Bigelow picked Bully up without incident and booked him at the county jail. Others said Bully missed the meal at Miss Lillian's house. What had happened to Miss Lillian? What was it like for poor Alice Fae having to endure the embarrassment of Bully's actions? What a poor example to set for young Jessie! Who was going to oversee Mr. John's farm during the critical harvest season?* Folks up and down the Ridge could not stop talking.

Two weeks passed with no activity on Mr. John's farm. Miss Lillian spent a few days in the hospital at Doc Grasson's suggestion, and Bully sat in jail. The bankers and cotton buyers in the county were restless with the fall harvest season ending. Mr. C.C. Bates, a powerful banker in Tupelo, the county seat of Lee County, sweated the most.

Fifteen hundred acres of cotton standing in the field can make for some strange circumstances. One afternoon, Mr. C.C. Bates and Mr. P.H. McDonald, a prominent cotton

buyer in the county, rode out to Miss Lillian's place. The two
men turned off the gravel road onto the long drive. They
encountered acres and acres of cotton, waiting to be
harvested. The chickens headed for cover. The black Cadillac
made its way toward the farmhouse. Although, Mr. John
Watson was a very prosperous farmer, he maintained a very
comfortable yet modest residence. Most of the resources
went back into the farm. Idle tractors and farm machinery
were seen down at the equipment shed. The two gentlemen
were met at the door by Alice Fae, who was busy washing
clothes when she heard the knock.

"Miss, my name is C.C. Bates, and this is Mr. P.H.
McDonald. We would like a word with the Lady of the
House, Miss Watson."

"Miss Lillian, there's some gentlemen here to see you,"
Alice Fae announced.

"Tell 'um to have a seat in the parlor," Miss Lillian
answered, She sounded almost like herself again.

"Can I get you a glass of tea?" Alice Fae asked; excited to
have someone in the house besides Miss Lillian.

"Yes, thank you," the two men responded in chorus.

Alice Fae disappeared toward the kitchen. The two men
took a seat.

The parlor was filled with antiques, which went well with
the hardwood floors. Over the fireplace was a large picture of
Francina in a gilded rococo frame. A beautiful Steinway piano
that Francina played sat in the corner. Only a new Victrola
betrayed the semblance of a parlor from the 1930s.

The two men rose and greeted the new widow when Miss
Lillian entered the room. They shared their heartfelt condolences, which were received, with graciousness. Miss Lillian
wore a simple blue cotton dress, her graying hair placed in
a bun.

"What do you two gentlemen want?" Miss Lillian asked; a slight edge to her voice.

She despised cotton buyers; bankers even more.

"As you know, Miss Watson, your husband, Mr. Watson maintained a long relation with the bank and died owing us a rather large sum of money," Mr. C.C. stated very businesslike. "To the point, we are concerned that our investment is in jeopardy. We are aware that no cotton was harvested the past two weeks."

"What happens on this farm is none of your business, you damn crook!" Miss Lillian exploded. She was back.

"On the contrary, Miss Watson, we have first mortgages on the crops and livestock, and a second mortgage on the farm equipment. Our institution has a vested interest in what happens out here, and we have one stipulation necessary to continue our relationship with you," Mr. C.C. retorted, digging in for the bank.

He was the largest stockholder. Mr. McDonald was the second largest stockholder.

"Stipulation? What damn stipulation, you low life?"

"We want you to put Bully in charge of running the farm." Mr. Bates spoke in his best banker tone.

"Over my dead body!"

Two large glasses of tea hit the floor in the hallway.

"Get the hell out of my house and don't you dare show your face around here, again!" Veins protruded from Miss Lillian's neck. She rose and pointed the two startled men to the door.

"Miss Lillian, listen to reason," Mr. McDonald spoke up, trying his luck.

"Like it or not, Bully, is the only one alive who knows enough about this farm to run it."

"Out! Out!" Miss Lillian fired back.

The two men backed out onto the front porch. Miss Lillian's one hundred ten-pound German Sheppard, Killer, came around the corner of the house to access the commotion.

Call it a reflex, nature, or just a bad habit, but when a German Shepard, named Killer, sees two bank stockholders running across a yard toward a strange black Cadillac, the primitive encoding in the DNA overrides any recent efforts toward domesticity. The cotton broker made it. The banker almost made it. When dealing with Killer, *almost* didn't count. Killer nailed Mr. C.C. in the ass when he attempted to climb into the passenger seat of the Cadillac. Killer drug the terrified banker from the car.

Bang!

Killer froze with his teeth dug into the banker's neck. The smell of gun powder permeated the air from Miss Lillian's 45 caliber pistol. Killer, eyes fixed, dared the banker to move.

"Killer let him go," Miss Lillian said. "Bates, get your hat and get this damn car outta my yard."

A slight smirk emanated from her face.

The distraught banker gathered up his hat and jumped into the Cadillac. His shorts hung out of a gaping hole in his hundred-dollar suit. Killer got an extra biscuit from Miss Lillian at supper.

———

Three days after Mr. C.C. Bates lost his dignity to a German Shepard, Sheriff Bigelow drove out to the Watson place. Horace Bigelow was a former student of Miss Lillian during her teaching days at Saltillo High. He had occupied the sheriff's office for the past four years. Prior to law enforcement, Sheriff

Bigelow was in the trucking business. He had lost so much money and was so in debt, to the powers that be, Mr. C.C. and Mr. McDonald, pooled their considerable influence and helped Horace win the election to the high sheriff post—a sure fire way to recoup their investment plus receive a residual benefit.

"Afternoon, Miss Lillian,"

He struggled to get his considerable girth dislodged from the new 1954 Pontiac.

Miss Lillian and Alice Fae shelled dried butter beans under an oak shade tree. Miss Lillian was cool toward the sheriff. This was not a social call.

"I heard you had some banker company out here a few days ago," Sheriff Bigelow said, tiptoeing up to the subject.

"Sheriff, if you're referring to that crook C.C. Bates and his crony, McDonald, yes," Miss Lillian flared.

"Now, don't get upset, Miss Lillian. We've got this little problem of what to do with Bully." The sheriff said.

Alice Fae did what she was best at doing: scooting down in her chair and pretending to be invisible.

"Sheriff, if you are coming out here with the same intentions as those two crooks, the day before yesterday, we don't have anything to talk about."

"I know you're mad at Bully, but he did not kill Mr. John, Miss Lillian," the Sheriff explained. "A run away mule wagon killed Mr. John. Besides, Bully is up there in my jail beating himself up more than you could ever do. It's killing him that Mr. John didn't forgive him before he died. He keeps saying over and over that he told Mr. John a hundred times that he was sorry, and he can't understand why Mr. John died without forgiving him. I told Bully that when you're busy dying, sometimes you just forget to do things."

"Sheriff, if I allow Bully to come back to the farm, would

you give me custody of him in return for not filing charges for his antics over at the church?" Miss Lillian questioned.

"Miss Lillian, I can't do that, but I'm sure Judge Claxton and the Mt. Zion deacons will cooperate in anything we decide. I just want to get this matter cleared up," the sheriff said.

"Sheriff, bring Bully to me tomorrow afternoon at three o'clock and I'll sign the necessary papers." Miss Lillian's eyes glared.

Alice Fae felt giddy about Bully coming home, but she never said anything.

———

Bully paced back and forth in his small cell; animal-like, He chewed his fingernails down to the quick and. now, he was going for second helpings. He read the newspaper accounts describing Mr. John's funeral; it all sounded foreign. He only recollected bits of the four days prior to Mr. John's funeral, and he had no memories of what he had done at Mt. Zion church.

Sheriff Bigelow walked into the jail block and rattled the huge iron door behind him.

"Bully, you interested in going home?"

"Sheriff, do termites love a sawmill?!" Bully shouted.

"Son, don't you be getting smart with me!" Sheriff Bigelow said.

"Yes, sir!" Bully folded an imaginary hat in his hand.

"You be ready to go tomorrow after lunch."

"Tomorrow? How about right now?"

"Tomorrow after lunch, Bully!" Sheriff Bigelow said. Bully bit into his nails.

The next afternoon, Sheriff Bigelow walked back into the

cell block with the keys of freedom in his hand. He pushed his weathered Stetson back on his huge head; he looked troubled.

"Come with me, Bully. You and me got to have a little talk."

"Yes, sir!" He giggled.

People talked about Sheriff Bigelow's office across the district. Law enforcement officers drove for miles, not to mention the locals, to see his famous roadkill collection. In collaboration with his unemployed brother-in-law, a taxidermist, the Sheriff had put together a staggering collection of possums, raccoons, bull frogs, squirrels, cats, dogs, foxes, snakes, and even a Holstein bull. He met his officers at the parking lot each evening to see what new critters the road had offered.

"Bully, I've worked out an arrangement with Judge Claxton, the deacons over at Mt. Zion church, and Miss Lillian. You can go home. You will have to pay for damages over at Mt. Zion, however."

"No problem, Sheriff. I just want to get home."

"Listen, Bully." His tone grew serious.

"The real reason I want you to get home is to help Miss Lillian get that crop outta the field. Do you think you can get the job done?"

"Yes, sir!"

"Get in my car and I'll take you out to Miss Lillian's place. She wants to see you."

When Bully walked to the Sheriff's car, Sheriff Bigelow called over to the bank.

"Mr. C.C., I just wanted to let you know the deal to return Bully to Miss Lillian's custody is final. And I plan to lean on him to get that crop outta the field, or else." The receiver clicked on the other end.

"Bully, you go ahead and get in the front seat and I'll get you down to Miss Lillian's," Sheriff Bigelow said.

"I can't believe I'm getting to go home, Sheriff."

After getting in the car, Sheriff Bigelow turned to Bully.

"I just want to say one thing to you, Bully. I can't tell you how important it is for you to come through and get that cotton outta the field this Fall; do you understand?"

"Yes, sir., I know I caused a lot of people a lot of trouble, and I want to make it up to them. I'm scared to death to look Miss Lillian in the eyes." Bully said.

"Bully let me say, if you let me down on this one, Miss Lillian will be the least of your problems. Do you understand me, son?" Sheriff Bigelow pulled his .38 Smith & Wesson and placed the blue barrel to Bully's throat.

"Yes, sir. I know I've been drinking too much. I'm going to straighten myself out and show you and Miss Lillian that I can be somebody. If Mr. John was still alive, he would be proud of what I'm about to do."

Sheriff Bigelow placed his pistol back into its holster and headed to the Watson place.

Sadness washed over Bully when they turned into the drive and drove toward Miss Lillian's. Memories of Mr. John swirled. The fear of Sheriff Bigelow and Miss Lillian was great, but it was overshadowed by Bully's loss.

Miss Lillian stood on the front porch when Sheriff Bigelow and Bully came to a stop. She waited for Bully. Even Sheriff Bigelow felt sorry for him, but not enough to stay very long. Miss Lillian met them getting out of the cruiser. Her eyes locked onto Bully and they never retreated.

"Thank you for being punctual, Sheriff. You can be leaving now. Bully and I need to have a private conversation."

The lines on Miss Lillian's face were deep and her jaw

locked. Her voice trembled. A small twitch developed under her left eye.

"I've got to be headed back to town, anyway, Miss Lillian. If I can help you in anyway, don't be bashful," Sheriff Bigelow said.

"I've never been accused of being bashful, Sheriff."

Bully and Miss. Lillian watched the sheriff get into his patrol car, make a wide turning swath across the yard and disappear in a huge column of dust.

Bully longed to be back in the safety of jail. The sound of a cocked pistol interrupted the silence.

"Bully, get moving toward the equipment shed or I will kill you on the spot—you decide."

"Please don't do anything rash, Miss Lillian. I'm moving."

Miss Lillian killed stray dogs at fifty yards with that same pistol. Bully witnessed her skills more than once. His mind raced with each step toward the shed. The thought to run gave way to a stark reality: death.

"Down the alley to the shop."

"Miss Lillian, whatever you do just don't hurt me,"

The alley was long, narrow and dark. It had a dirt floor. Faint slivers of sunlight filtered through the dust particles, creating light and shadows. When Bully and Miss Lillian approached the doorway of the shop. Bully heard the sound only old timers could describe: the sound of high tensile steel jaws, springing from the earth, flying toward each other only to find the foot of some unfortunate animal impeding their connection, or in this case, Bully's leg. A bear trap's first insult crushes an animal's leg. The second one produces such a grip that no escape is possible. She had secured the trap with the heaviest chain on the farm.

"Augh!" Bully screamed. He fell to the floor and grabbed his leg. Blood, dirt, spit and urine mixed in a grizzly concoction. Bully's body withered in agony. The sound of chain links becoming taut and releasing mixed with eerie moans echoing down the darken hallway.

Miss Lillian smiled.

"Revenge can be so sweet," she whispered to herself.

Miss Lillian cocked her pistol and pointed it toward Bully's head.

"I'm going to release this chain and you better drag yourself down this hall to the tool shop."

"Miss Lillian, please don't kill me. Why did you do this?"

"I'll tell you why, you son of a bitch." Her left eye began to twitch.

"You took John away from me. After you came along, I never saw John. You were his complete focus. 'Bully this. Bully that.' He pushed me to the side; before you, we were inseparable. I thought about drowning you in the bathtub after that bitch mother of yours left; wish I had, now. But at least she left."

Her voice softened, and a small smile replaced her frown. She repositioned the grease bucket back in its designated spot and walked back to the farmhouse. She called the cotton gin and two of the farm hands took Bully over to Doc Grasson's.

———

Jessie arrived from school, startled to find his mother at home.

"Hey, sweetheart. How was your day?"

"Mamma, what are you doing home? I can't wait to see Daddy!"

This was a new experience for Jessie. His excitement radiated. Alice Fae prepared a meal of boiled cabbage, ham hocks, and cornbread for Bully; his favorite. She moved around the house, dusting and cleaning, wanting everything to be neat. Four o'clock. Five o'clock. Seven o'clock. The sun set. Bully never showed. By nine thirty, with the meal cold, Alice Fae spotted two headlights making their way down the small trail to the "little house" on Mr. John's farm--the farm manager's house. Alice Fae ran out on the porch and saw Doc Grasson's green Chevy pickup pull into the yard. His expression communicated trouble. Alice Fae knew it was Bully.

"Alice Fae, Bully's hurt," Doc said.

"What happened?! Is he alive?!"

"Yeah. He's alive, but he may never walk right again. He's in the truck."

Alice Fae ran toward the truck. Jessie came running and jumped off the porch into Doc's arms.

"Not now, son. Your dad's hurt. Help me get him into the house."

Bully moved in and out of consciousness with the help of Doc Grasson's private morphine inventory. Doc instructed Alice Fae to prepare a bed, and he coached Jessie on how to help him move Bully from the truck.

THE TELEGRAM

The Trailways bus pulled into the station. Francina looked for her mother. The telegram she received was abrupt and final. FRANCINA, COME HOME. STOP. YOUR FATHER HAS BEEN KILLED IN AN ACCIDENT. STOP. She withdrew from the conservatory and caught the USS United Steamer to New York.

Francina possessed remarkable beauty. Her long red hair and porcelain like complexion turned many heads. She appeared out of place in the backwoods of Mississippi. Miss Lillian compensated with the finest clothes and many trips to Memphis, New Orleans, and Jackson. She introduced Francina to opera, musicals, art, and a way of life few people between Euclatubba and Jug Fork knew. Francina remembered the field hand's curiosity when a truck rolled in from Memphis with her huge Steinway piano, the only one in Lee County.

High seas from London to New York were treacherous, but secondary to Francina's grief. She regretted the lack of closeness between her and her father. They had tried to improve their relationship but with little success. Miss Lillian's presence and pervasive focus on Francina's life left little room for another major relationship. After many awkward attempts, they quit trying. Mr. John expressed quiet approval with each passing year. Francina gained confidence and increased recognition with her music. He attended most of the 4-H talent contests and beauty contests Miss Lillian always found, whether in Memphis, Natchez, or wherever. When Francina attended Ole Miss, Miss Lillian and Mr. John drove over to Oxford for her recitals. Mr. John felt awkward in those settings. He tagged along while Miss Lillian forged ahead in total command of any situation.

When the bus pulled into its berth, Francina spotted her mother and Betty Mae. They stood near the blue Oldsmobile Mr. John gave her mother for Christmas two years ago. Francina bolted off the bus.

"Mother! Tell me this is not happening. Daddy can't be dead. He's in the fields; tell me he is in the fields!" Tears poured.

Miss Lillian cried along with Francina; the two embraced. Betty Mae became tearful and joined in. The three women were oblivious to the curious passengers who moved around the sobbing threesome to retrieve their luggage.

On the way home, Miss Lillian and Betty Mae brought Francina up to date with events of the past three weeks. Though out of the way, Francina wanted to visit her father's grave at Mt. Zion Cemetery. Miss Lillian obliged her but not because she wanted to.

THE MOVE

Jessie's dog, Rover, barked as the old Diamond T stake truck approached Bully and Alice Fae's house. God was showing off his splendor with one of those beautiful Fall days in Mississippi. The sun rose over the open cotton fields and the dew dripped off the honeysuckle along the fence rows. Young field rabbits played near the road. The morning temperature cooled, hinting of the coming winter, but it faded by ten o'clock and turned hot by noon.

Bully spent a fitful night and Alice Fae never slept. Doc Grasson instructed her to bathe the wound with some godawful concoction every two hours. Alice Fae dozed off on the sofa until, she heard Rover and the engine of the Diamond T. She shook the sleep off and gazed out the window. Jarvis and Cleo, field hands sent by Miss Lillian, approached the porch. Alice Fae met them at the door.

"Miss Alice Fae, Miss Lillian sent us over to help you and Mr. Bully move."

"Move! Jarvis, what are you talking about? And put your hat back on your head!"

"Miss Alice, I don't know nothing except Miss Lillian told us to be here at daylight and hep you and Mr. Bully move over to the Vinson place."

"The Vinson place! No one has lived in that shack for years. It's a dump!"

"Look, Miss Alice, we don't want no trouble. She told me and Cleo to help y'all move and we gotta help y'all move. We don't want to get on Miss Lillian's bad side."

Alice Fae let them in, and they dismantled her world right before her eyes. Within two hours, trip after trip, to the truck, they transformed the "little house" into an empty box. Bully was oblivious.

"Jarvis, please be careful with that dresser. It was my mamma's."

"Yes, we being as careful as a mamma cow with her newborn." The dresser crashed into the truck with Alice Fae's other possessions. The last two pieces of furniture were Jessie and Bully's bed.

"Miss Alice, we got to move and in a hurry. We shoulda been in them fields an hour ago. Miss Lillian drove down them rows of nigger shacks, yestiddy late, blowing that horn and shooting that pistol in the air, screaming and hollering. She said everybody better be picking cotton when that sun came up. The party is over, Miss Alice Fae. We gotta go."

Alice entered the empty room where Jessie slept.

"Honey, honey," She nudged Jessie. "Sweetie, you got to wake up. We got to go for a ride."

Jessie brushed the sleep from his eyes. He reached up and gave her a hug.

"Come on, now. Get your clothes on. Put your old ones on, honey. You don't have to go to school today."

Jessie jumped out of his bed and grinned. "Mamma, where's the furniture?"

"Honey, we got to move. It's in the Diamond T out in the front yard. Just get your clothes on and don't ask questions."

"Mamma, how's daddy's foot?"

"I hope it's okay, Jessie. I don't know for sure. Now, no more questions." She approached Bully. "Wake up, Bully, I need you to wake up."

Bully muttered something inaudible and appeared semi-conscious. The steady stream of morphine from Doc Grasson had worked. Alice Fae instructed Jarvis and Cleo to load Bully into the front seat of the Diamond T. She squeezed in next to Bully's limp body. His head fell on her shoulder. Jessie and Cleo straddled the giant teardrop headlights, which set on the fenders of the Diamond T. Rover jumped off the porch and landed on Alice Fae's mamma's dresser. The Diamond T. left the manager's house and drove to the Vinson place.

———

Rumors flew at the Jug Fork general store after Bully got out of jail. Old, worn out men sat around checkers and domino tables discussing politics, current events, the weather, and other people's business. This was a good day for gossip. A small shower developed and people, rescued from the fields, trickled in replenishing the pipeline with new information and hearsay.

Jarvis stopped by to fix a flat tire. He hunkered over the slick tire. Sweat dripped off his nose and fell to the dusty rim. His Prince Albert tobacco kept falling out of his bib overalls. He was in a foul mood. Harold Pepper, one of the regular fixtures on the front porch of the Jug Fork store. He could glean information with the best of them.

Harold always opened with a statement.

"Jarvis, I hear Bully ran into a little bad luck and hurt his foot."

"Where did you hear that?" Jarvis always replied with a question.

"Man rode through on a horse saying he heard it.," Harold said, bringing out his knight.

"What color horse was it?" Jarvis brought out his knight, too.

"Folks down at the church said they heard the same thing. Even heard the preacher comment on it," Harold said, bringing out his bishop.

"That preacher hasn't listened to our preacher, has he?" Jarvis responded with his bishop.

"Jarvis, they said even Miss Lillian commented on Bully's accident over the party line the other day." Harold responded with his queen amid mounting frustration.

"Have you asked Miss Lillian your own self?" Jarvis played his queen.

"Shit, Jarvis! You're 'bout as much fun as that damn blind dog that my wife won't let me shoot."

Jarvis grinned.

Stalemate.

———

Bully woke the following morning disoriented and in excruciating pain.

"Alice Fae! Alice Fae! Damn it! I'm dying!"

Rover heard the commotion and ambled in the front door.

He buried his nose into Bully's crotch.

"Rover knock it off! I'm dying! Where are you, Alice Fae?"

If Rover could have talked, he would have told Bully that

Miss Lillian sent one of the field hands for Alice Fae. Miss Francina had a ton of laundry and besides, Alice Fae hadn't worked the previous afternoon.

Bully panned the room: cardboard boxes nailed to the walls, the ceiling fallen in, vines grew through broken windowpanes, and bricks fell from the fireplace into a heap. Bully looked down and noticed the dusty earth between wide cracks in the flooring.

Bully sank back into the old couch. The pain took away any initiative to give a damn, when in walked Willard.

"Nice place y'all got here, Bully." Willard took a long slow drink of Wild Cat whiskey from a pint Mason jar, careful to avoid a chip in its lip.

Now Willard was... different. He was long and lanky, his jeans hung, and his shirt was unbuttoned, revealing his hairless chest and protruding ribs. He had dish water blond hair. His two front teeth were missing, and he wore an ankle length blue coat, winter or summer.

"Where the hell am I, Willard?" Bully got back to his original question.

"Peers to me, you've been demoted and rel-i-gated to an outpost on the far fringes of Miss Lillian's vast empire, son."

"Cut the crap, Willard! Where am I?"

"Well, let's say... it's not the Ritz." He held his sides and chuckled.

"Willard!"

"The Vinson place."

"The Vinson place! Jesus Christ!"

Bully tried to kick a magazine rack with his good foot.

"Give me a drink of whatever your drinking!"

"You man enough to handle it?"

"I'll drink you under the table any day, you toothless asshole!" Bully yelled, taking the Mason jar. Bully leaned forward when his eye caught a bright glint in Willard's mouth.

"Do I see what I think I see?"

"Yep, my gold tooth! After six months with Mr. Carl, you get a gold tooth. It marks you as one of his boys." Willard pulled back his lip revealing his golden left canine.

"Well, at least you'll never be broke."

Bully gulped the clear white liquid, which flowed out of the hills in Northern Mississippi.

"Jesus! Where did you git this stuff?"

"Made it myself. What do you think?"

"What do I think? How can I think while I'm on fire?!" Bully took another long drink.

On the record, people didn't drink in north Mississippi in 1954. Off the record, if you wanted it, you could get it. Bootlegging was big business. Bully met Willard through Mr. John. Mr. John rented a farm from one of the largest bootleggers in Lee County, Carl Butcher. Willard, who worked for Mr. Carl, would bring Mr. John a sample of the latest batch from time to time, courtesy of Mr. Carl. Bully and Willard just hit it off.

"So, how's farming?" Willard asked, flashing his gold tooth.

"Shut up! This has been the worst month in my life. I keep thinking things got to git better, but they ain't. I sure miss Mr. John. I can't get him off my mind. It's messing me up, Willard. It's messing me up real bad." Bully took another drink. He didn't notice the pain in his foot anymore.

"Shit, boy! You need cheering up. Git yourself together and let's go for a ride."

"Suits me, anything to get outta this dump."

Bully got up and the pain pushed through the whiskey.

"Augh! Damn!" Bully twisted, buried his head in the sofa and bit into the worn fabric.

"Easy, buddy. Let me help you."

After a long silence, Bully regained some of his composure.

"I never thought I'd be asking you for help, Willard."

Bully knew he shouldn't be moving around, but his heart hurt more than his foot. He needed relief. He didn't care where it came from. Willard, with some effort, helped Bully into his old black Ford pickup, and they drove away from the shack on the Vinson place. Bully, looking through the dirty side mirror, saw Rover sitting on the porch guarding Alice Fae's mamma's dresser.

TWENTY-MILE BOTTOM

Twenty-mile Bottom was a raccoon's paradise. On the north end, a six inch Artesian well rose out of the ground with a continuous flow of water that flooded the wooded bottom land for miles and miles. Twenty-mile Bottom was filled with cypress, oak, sweet gum and cottonwood trees.

Willard and Bully left the Vinson place, turned east and headed for Twenty-mile Bottom. The sun was at ten o'clock.

Bully continued to drink the Wild Cat whiskey, making him oblivious to the pain in his foot. Folks between Euclatubba and Jug Fork thought anything East of Saltillo was backwards. Twenty-mile Bottom was East of Saltillo.

Bully felt giddy, like he was skipping school. Willard's Ford made its way around the tight curves. Bully could feel the cool breeze and the warm sun on his face. Hank Williams blared from the radio; that coat hanger for an antenna didn't look all that good, but it was doing the job. Wagons, with cotton heaped high, were parked at the edge of the fields. Willard looked over at Bully and smiled a gold toothed grin.

Bully couldn't help but laugh. He had not laughed in a long time.

"Let's go over to the old sawmill site and shoot the guns," Willard suggested.

"Sounds good to me. It just feels good to get out." Bully liked Willard leading, drunk or sober. He just wanted to tag along.

By the time they reached the old mill site, Willard was intoxicated. He started to drink with his cornflakes. Willard stopped the truck, opened the door, and fell out into the rotten sawdust that covered the ground around the mill site.

"Boy, that's good whiskey!" Willard slurred, He staggered to his feet.

"You ought to slow up a bit, Willard. We got to git home."

"Shit, boy! Don't start getting righteous on me! This is our day off!"

Willard took another drink, and surveyed the scene. He stumbled around to Bully's side of the truck and stuck his head in the window. Deep furrows in his brow revealed a very serious expression on his face.

"Bully, can I ask you a personal question?"

"Sure, Willard. What?"

"I mean a personal, personal question? He got even closer.

Bully saw blood vessels in the whites of his eyes and smelled the Wild Cat whiskey on his hot breath.

"Sure, Willard. You and me are friends. What is it?

"Have you ever fucked a farm animal?"

"Jesus! Willard! Shut up! Your drunk." Bully jerked away, hitting his head on the rear-view mirror, knocking it down into the floorboard. Bully found himself a bit more sober.

"No, I'm serious." Willard's patented goofy look crossed his face.

"Hell, no. To answer your question."

"Hand me my rifle."

"Willard, what the hell are you thinking?"

"Just hand me the rifle."

Bully knew Willard, whiskey, and guns didn't mix.

He's a wild boar at a prayer meeting, Willard thought.

The old mill site was once a prosperous sawmill owned by the Langford brothers. They moved in, cut thousands of cypress trees from the bottom, then moved on. The dilapidated mill shed, the slab pile, and the mountain of sawdust were the only remnants.

Willard took a prone position across the hood of the old Ford and took a bead across the mill site.

"What are you aiming for, Willard?

"A chicken."

"A chicken? What chicken?"

Bully looked in the direction of Willard's intentions. Near the fringe of the clearing, a big red hen and several chicks scratched in the sawdust.

"Willard, don't shoot that chicken."

"This is something I've always wanted to try."

His rifle wobbled. Willard's cocked eye struggled to zero in on his prey.

"Don't tell me what I'm thinking."

"Fuck a chicken," Willard slurred.

Bang!

Bully jerked. Willard hit the chicken. The bullet passed through the poor animal's leg and she flopped around on the ground. The chicks scattered. Pitiful squawks echoed through the woods. Willard threw the rifle down, staggered across the sawmill site and lunged for the wounded chicken. She flopped. Willard dove. The chicken darted. Willard zigged. The chicken zagged. Willard geed. The chicken hawed. The drunk Willard, with a diving lunge that would have made any football coach proud, made a spectacular move and grabbed the chicken by her good leg.

Bully was in disbelief. He laughed at Willard and cried for the chicken, all at the same time. Willard got up, huffing and puffing, and staggered back to the Ford. He carried the flopping chicken by the feet. Sawdust ran down his pant legs.

"Let her go, Willard! You had your fun."

"Hell, no. I'm going to see if what I have heard all my life is true."

"What?"

"That there is nothing like fucking a chicken." "Jesus! You're sick, Willard! That damn whiskey has gone straight to your head, Willard."

"Sorry, we only have one chicken, Bully too bad."

"Willard, leave me alone. It's my day off."

Bully poured another Mason jar of Wild Cat. Willard held on to the side of the truck with one hand and clutched the struggling chicken in the other. Bully watched through the side mirror. Willard dropped his pants. Bully took a drink, slid down in the seat, and turned the radio to maximum volume.

"Hey, good looking. What ya got cooking? I got a hotrod Ford and a two-dollar bill..."

The truck shook, and the gut wrenching shriek of the tortured chicken drowned out the music. The shaking stopped, and Willard let out a yell, echoing down the bottom. The chicken's head, detached from its body, hit the top of the Ford and slid down the windshield, leaving a bloody trail.

Bully grabbed his stomach, lunged for the open window, and wasted his Wild Cat down the side of the truck.

Willard passed out with his headless chicken.

———

Bully missed supper. By the time Willard awoke, he'd gotten a terrible sunburn on his privates. He passed out in the back of the Ford and had been there for three hours.

Willard created a terrible situation for himself. His naked and battered body ached from severe sunburn. He abandoned all modesty and sought comfort. They made progress toward Jug Fork until Willard saw the red light and heard the siren of Sheriff Bigelow's vigilant deputy. Willard pulled over, and the deputy approached.

"Willard, I need you to get out of the truck."

"You see I'm in an awkward situation, James."

"You need to show me some respect, Willard, and get out of the truck."

"Yes, sir!" Willard exited the truck to the contorted facial expression of the deputy.

"I got to call for backup."

"Backup, what the hell do you need backup for?"

The deputy retreated to his car and sounded the alarm.

Before the ordeal ended, there were fifteen to twenty patrol cars around the old Ford. Willard's interest in poultry faded along with the sun on his special day off.

JESSIE'S PIANO LESSONS

Miss Francina possessed more clothes than most Southern families combined. They all needed to be washed. Alice Fae separated the clothes in piles across the back porch: colored ones, white ones, delicate ones, miscellaneous ones. Miss Lillian's new ringer washing machine clanked in high gear. By noon, God's clothes dryer made a dent in the mountain of clothes.

Miss Lillian insisted on using soap made on the farm. Mr. John always killed ten hogs after the first frost. His crew placed the fat taken from the hogs and put it in huge black pots. When cooked, the fat produced grease. The grease, with Merry War Lye, created a concoction that when cooled, became soap. When cut into squares, it created a year's supply of general-purpose soap. Special hand soap, made by a mixture of general-purpose soap mix and corn cob ashes, completed the day. Alice Fae enjoyed a special relationship with the soap she sprinkled into each wash. She helped make it.

Miss Lillian and Francina spent most of the day in the

parlor catching up on details of Mr. John's tragic accident, the future of the farm, Europe, relatives, etc. Alice Fae, ghost like, remained in the background; there, but not heard or seen. All the while, she missed nothing. She possessed an uncanny ability to expect Miss Lillian's moods. Perfected over the years, she become chameleon like.

Alice Fae struggled to stay awake. Up at all hours the night before with Bully and a move, she felt spent. Also, she worried about Bully.

"Alice Fae!" Every cell in Alice Fae's body exploded into upright attention.

"Yes'um!"

"Come in here!" Miss Lillian demanded. Alice Fae entered the parlor where Francina and Miss Lillian were having coffee.

"Tell me about Jessie, Alice Fae," Francina asked.

"What do you want to know?" Alice Fae straitened her hair and dress.

"What's he interested in? How's he doing in school?" Miss Lillian appeared bored.

"Miss Francina, he's a wonderful little boy. He's my pride and joy. He loves to read, chase rabbits, throw rocks, and bark like a dog. You know, all those boy things," Alice Fae glowed.

"Listen, Alice Fae. One of my courses of instruction at the conservatory focused on the techniques of teaching music. It gave me all kinds of ideas. But I have a problem. I need a student. I wonder if Jessie might like to take piano lessons."

"Oh, Miss Francina! That's wonderful!"

"You have to make sure he's cleaned up before he comes into this house!" Miss Lillian said.

"Mother!" Francina's face flashed disapproval.

"Send Jessie to see me tomorrow afternoon after school and we will see if he's interested."

Alice Fae swelled with excitement. For a moment, she

forgot her exhaustion. Alice Fae gathered her belongings and turned toward the back porch.

"Alice Fae, where is Bully today?" Miss Lillian asked.

"Bully hurt his foot somehow, Miss Lillian. You should see it. It's awful. He's down at our new place you were *kind* enough to give us," Alice Fae said.

"You tell him I want to see him, foot and all, in what is now *my* office in the morning at six o'clock. I'll send Jarvis after him."

Miss Lillian knew he couldn't walk. "Yes, ma'am."

———

Doc Grasson dropped by Bully's new place after hearing he had moved. He wanted another look at his foot and to drop off a few more days' worth of morphine. Doc feared Bully might lose his foot without proper medical care. Bully refused to go to the hospital. Doc found Rover on the porch still guarding Alice Fae's mamma's dresser, but no Bully.

Alice Fae turned the corner and headed for her new home. The sun faded. The walk from the "Big House" to her new place was now about three miles. When she entered the drive, Jarvis and Cleo met her in the Diamond T. They had dropped Jessie off and were headed home. Jessie assisted in the fields after school, during cotton harvest. Jarvis and Cleo waved. No one spoke; they were too tired. Jessie met his exhausted mother with excitement, a cartwheel, and a hug.

"Where's Daddy?"

"What do you mean? Isn't he in the house?"

"Nope."

"Well, that's not good. He doesn't need to be on that foot."

"How did Daddy hurt his foot, Mamma?

"I don't know. I tried to ask him last night, but he was so out of it that he didn't make a bit of sense.

"Maybe he was fighting a bear."

"Well, whatever he was fighting, might as well have been a bear. Come in the house and let's get some tea. I've got something to ask you."

"What, Mamma! What?"

"Let me catch my breath, get some tea, and we'll talk."

Alice Fae looked at the total chaos surrounding her: the hanging ceiling, the swaying floors, and the broken windowpanes. Her spirit faded, and the broken home's image blurred through her tears. Her thoughts turned to Jessie, Bully, Mavis, and Rover; she shook the feelings off. She turned away from Jessie and poured two large jelly glasses full of sassafras tea. Alice Fae, tea in hand, headed for the swing on the front porch. Jessie followed.

"Jessie, sit by me and let's enjoy our tea and this nice breeze. I have something I want to ask you."

"What, Mamma, what?"

"Jessie, do you like music?"

"Like church singing and stuff?"

"Well, kind of but not hardly. No particular kind of music. Just music. I notice you sing to yourself a lot." "Yeah, Mamma. Why?"

"Well, Miss Francina is back from overseas, and she wants to know if you'd like to learn to play the piano."

"Whoa! Tell her, yes! Double yes!"

Jessie had a tremendous crush on Miss Francina. She was always polite and nice to him.

He would have signed up for anything she taught.

———

Alice Fae banged plates and saucers into the crude cabinets. Cold beans and corn bread sat on the stove. Lights appeared around the curve and approached the house. It was Bully and Willard. Alice Fae seethed and her mind raced.

Bully shouldn't be on that foot. If he felt good enough to go out, he felt good enough to work around the house, she thought. Jessie tried staying up until his daddy got home. He wanted to tell him about the music lessons, but he fell asleep.

Bully's whiskey and morphine were depleted. Each bump in the road reminded him of his pain. Willard stopped at the cotton gin and got a flour sack to protect his privates. The thought of a social encounter repulsed Willard. He pulled to a near stop by the porch, offered Bully no help. Bully stumbled out of the truck and grabbed the porch railing.

Willard drove away.

Bully hobbled in, still drunk, but he could feel the chill Alice Fae cast in his direction.

"What's your problem?" Bully said.

"Nothing."

"Nothing, huh?"

"Bully, you shouldn't have gone out today, and you know it."

"Don't be telling me what I outta be doing, Alice Fae! I got enough people telling me what to do. I sure don't need another 'un." Bully said..

"Well, Miss Lillian wants to see you at six o'clock in the morning. Sounds serious. I don't know how you're going to work on that foot. But we got to eat."

"Look, bitch, I don't see anybody going hungry around her. So, why don't you just shut the hell up!"

Jessie, in the adjoining room, heard his mother and father yelling. He remembered his music lessons. He came out with his pillow, squinting his eyes from the light.

"Daddy."

"Jessie, get back in the bed," Alice Fae said.

"Daddy, I wanted to tell you about my piano lessons."

"Piano lessons! No boy of mine is gonna take no sissified piano lessons!" Bully came out of the seat.

"But, Daddy, Miss Fran"

Wham! Bully backhanded Jessie across the face. His frail sixty-seven pounds went flying into a pile of boxes.

"Bully! Don't!" Alice Fae screamed.

Bully half hobbled, and half staggered across the room, taking his belt off. He grabbed Jessie by the hair and began to beat him. Jessie screamed and tried to protect himself but was no match for his drunken father. The leather cut into Jessie's flesh with each blow from his powerful, work hardened arms. His arm tired. He switched hands with no loss of effect. He did not relent.

Alice Fae ran through the house, hysterical. She pleaded, screamed, prayed, ran to the porch, and then back into the house.

"Stop, Bully! Please, stop!"

The only response was the sound of leather on flesh. Then silence.

Bully threw his belt across the room, went to a small churn where he kept his whiskey and found a half pint. He took the lid off, emptied it and threw the empty bottle across the room toward the belt. He hobbled off the porch, reeking of whiskey, pants sagging, and foot aching. He faded into the darkness.

DOC GRASSON'S GIFT

The sun rose. A foggy mist hung low, drenching the Mississippi world of Johnson grass, morning glories, cotton, magnolias and pecan trees in a wet, dripping blanket of dew. The faithful rooster's crow carried across the land beckoning the new day.

The rooster's crow startled Bully from a deep sleep.

Where the hell am I, he thought.

On two consecutive mornings, this question confronted Bully. He struggled to wake. He opened one eye and saw the vague shape of a corn sheller and heard the unmistakable rooting and grunting sounds of pigs. His foot throbbed with pain. He opened his other eye, and a thought occurred: *this could be a corn crib.* Turning, he focused on fifteen to twenty small pigs. They seized the opportunity of the open door, scooted past Bully and headed for hog heaven; seven hundred bushels of unguarded corn.

Bully's mind returned to the following day. He remembered the first half well, but the second half blurred. He could remember bits and pieces: an argument with Alice Fae and...

"Oh, shit!" Bully yelled. "I'm supposed to be at Miss Lillian's at six this morning!"

Bully's sudden alarm startled the feeding pigs. A fury of porcine mass stampeded for the door. Bully lay in the door. He tried to get up but failed. Five seconds of chaos, followed by a blinding pain from his foot, left him in agony. He teetered on the threshold of unconsciousness but refused the luxury; he needed to make Miss Lillian's meeting.

Why hogs defecate when excited took on more than an academic curiosity for Bully. Between the pain and the pig shit, Bully knew his day would get better. It didn't.

————

Jarvis walked into a hurricane when he stepped into Miss Lillian's office without Bully. Jarvis thought, *I'd rather castrate a two thousand-pound bull than tell Miss Lillian that Bully's missing.* Jarvis entered Mr. John's office.

Miss Lillian sat at John's former desk.

"What did I tell you to do?"

Jarvis's wilted body language told the whole story. Before Jarvis opened his mouth, Miss Lillian answered her question with another one.

"Well, where the hell is he?"

"Miss Lillian, all I know is Miss Alice Fae said he wasn't there, and she didn't know."

Bully walked in.

"Where in Satan have you been?"

Bully washed up the best he could in a horse trough down at the barn and found an empty flour sack to dry himself off. He half limped, half swaggered into the office. Late or not, Bully knew Miss Lillian needed him to oversee the harvest.

"Jarvis, get to the cotton field!"

"Yes'um, Miss Lillian."

Jarvis winked at Bully on his way out.

————

Alice Fae didn't sleep the night of Jessie's beating. When Jarvis came for Bully, he found her on the front porch swing, fetal like, staring out across the cotton field. She sent him on his way with no recollection of their conversation. She tried to comfort Jessie through the night. A busted lip and twenty to thirty cuts and bruises crisscrossed his back, hips, and legs. All night, Jessie muttered and took the blame. He rocked, talked to himself, and rocked.

"If I hadn't wanted to take piano lessons, Daddy wouldn't have gotten mad," he said.

"Honey don't talk about it. Just push those thoughts away, far away. Think about ole Rover."

Alice Fae looked down the drive fearful Bully would return. Rover barked. She jumped.

This is Willard's fault. Bully's not mean until he gets with Willard, she thought.

She hated Willard.

————

After two weeks of being "shut down," Miss Lillian's attitude and vision cleared. She decided to take personal charge of the farming empire Mr. John left behind. No "hired hand" deserved or was entitled to the job. *To hell with what C.C. Bates wanted.* The thought of C.C. Bates lit a fire in the old woman. She rose at four-thirty each morning and everyone on the farm was in the fields by six-thirty. She demanded it.

Mr. John's office was large. It attached to the equipment

shed Bully built. Mr. John placed him in charge of building the most modern equipment shed in the county. Bully took great pride in Mr. John's trust, and he came through with excellence. People from Mississippi State drove up from Starkville to see it. The folks from Rock City, Tennessee, wanted to paint their sign on the roof. Entering the office door, the beautiful knotty pine paneling impressed. Mr. John filled his backwall with a lifetime of awards and pictures. Mr. John's pride and joy was his picture with Senator John Stennis. Every democratic candidate who campaigned in Lee County knocked on Mr. John's door. Along the walls were hundreds of eighteen-inch brown paper tubes with cotton protruding from each end, called cotton samples. A grade was given to each sample, which determined the price paid for each five-hundred-pound bail of cotton. Mr. John's massive roll top desk sat on the right wall, with scores of drawers, nooks, shelves, and slots. A picture of Miss Lillian and Francina occupied the top on one side. There were several deer heads and one bear head mounted on the front wall; Sheriff Bigelow's brother-in-law's work.

"Sit down, Bully!" Miss Lillian said..

He hobbled over to a cane bottom chair next to Mr. John's desk and eased down with a grimace.

"Bully, I don't have a lot of time to mess with you this morning," Miss Lillian said..

"From our little conversation, day before yesterday, you are aware that I don't care for you that much--never have. What John saw in you is a mystery to me."

Bully sank lower and lower in his chair with each word.

"Some people think I should turn this place over to you; that won't happen." Miss Lillian's eyes flashed.

"Bully, if you and I are to work together, you will have to go back to zero and work your way into my good graces."

Bully's eyes lit for a moment.

"I've decided to let you be Curtis's assistant, working the livestock."

"Curtis's assistant! I hate livestock, and Curtis is an idiot!" Bully blurted.

"Until you hear from me, you are not to operate any farm equipment or be seen in the fields. Do you understand me?"

"Yes, ma'am."

Bully was devastated. He lived, slept, and breathed to be in the fields atop a huge tractor.

"Now, git outta here! And report to Curtis. I've got work to do." Miss Lillian turned away and shuffled through a stack of papers.

Bully stood in shock. Stunned. Within four minutes, he had moved from the heir apparent farm manager to an idiot's assistant. He hobbled toward the door.

"Bully, you do what Curtis says or you will regret the day. And another thing: no damn field hand is leading us out of this mess John left. I'm doing it!"

Bully slammed the screen door on his way out.

———

"Mavis! Mavis!"

"Alice Fae, what are you doing out so early?"

"Mavis, Bully went wild on Jessie last night. He and that low life Willard went off yesterday and got drunk. Bully came home last night raising cane and whipped Jessie senseless." Alice Fae's voice cracked, and her lips quivered.

"I'll kill them both," Mavis said.

"Jessie is like my own. It's one thing to go off on someone your own size, but not little Jessie. That ain't right, Alice Fae!"

"It's that Willard, Mavis. Bully would be all right if it wasn't for Willard."

"I got a bullet for that Willard, but no one held a gun on Bully, Alice Fae," Mavis pointed her index finger.

"No, Mavis. I just need you to help me with Jessie today. Miss Lillian is looking for me right now, I bet."

"You don't fret your head 'bout nothing, girl. Me and Jessie will be just fine."

"Oh, thank you, Mavis!" Alice Fae hugged Mavis.

"Can he get down here on his own?"

"Yeah, I think so. He's just real sore." Alice Fae paused.

"There's something else I sure need your thoughts on."

"What is it?"

"Miss Francina offered to teach Jessie piano lessons, and Jessie got all excited. When he told Bully 'bout it, he went off. She wants to talk with Jessie at three o'clock this afternoon. I'm afraid Bully might go off on Jessie again, if we go ahead. What do you think?"

"If that little boy wants to take up piano lessons, I say let him. That's my two cents on it."

"You don't think it might happen again?" Alice Fae replied.

"Can't go around scared all your life, Alice Fae."

"Guess you're right. Will you make sure Jessie gets up to Miss Francina's?"

"You can count on me, Alice Fae."

———

Doc Grasson woke with Bully on his mind.

He's in trouble with his foot under the best of circumstances. Time's short. But, why am I chasing all over the country looking for

Bully? It's not my foot. He's the one refusing to go to the hospital. How did he get injured? Why could I not get a straight answer?

He finished breakfast, grabbed his hat, and headed down to the Watson place.

Alice Fae hurried, got Jessie over to Mavis's and prayed to avoid hell from Miss Lillian. She felt exhausted. Alice Fae hurried along the road to Miss Lillian's, deep in fear and thought. A vehicle interrupted. Doc Grasson's green Chevy appeared around the curved gravel road. He recognized her and slowed to a stop.

"Good morning, Alice Fae. How are you this morning?" She hesitated. One word might start an avalanche of tears.

"Fine, Doc. How are you?"

"You sure, Alice Fae?"

"Yes sir. I'm just a little tired."

"Where could I find Bully this morning? I'm worried about his foot."

Alice Fae worried more about his head.

"He's supposed to meet with Miss Lillian first thing this morning. You might catch him there."

"Are you headed that way?"

"Yes, sir."

"If that's the case, get in and I'll give you a ride."

"That's mighty nice of you, Doc Grasson."

Alice Fae moved around to the passenger side and climbed in. Doc Grasson turned around and drove for Miss Lillian's place.

"How did Bully hurt that foot, Alice Fae?"

"Your guess is good as mine, Doc. He won't tell me."

"Strange. How's Jessie?"

"Fine."

"Does he like to read?"

"Oh, yes, sir." Her voice brightened.

"I've got a few books he might like. Next time I'm headed this way, I'll drop them off."

"What kinda books, Doc Grasson?"

"Civil War books."

"Oh, I'm sure he would like that, Doc. He's such a good boy."

Doc Grasson occupied the local expert chair on the Civil War. He could extol for days. His grandfather fought with Barksdale's Mississippi regiment at Fredericksburg. Doc Grasson had walked the battlefields of Brice's Cross Roads, Gettysburg, Fredericksburg, and Shiloh and made the terrain and stories come alive with his detailed descriptions of the battles. Since his wife, Miss Olga, died in nineteen forty-two, he spent most of his free time studying the great battles and the cast of characters that had decided the ultimate outcome of the epic struggle. He never remarried.

————

God created Curtis simple. Nineteen years old and over-weight, he operated with the brain and personality of a child. Rudy complexion and bucktoothed, his pants forever sagged. His thoughts were concrete and devoid of insight. Mr. John struggled to find a place for him. He tried him on a tractor. Curtis crashed into a cotton wagon and killed a mule before the dinner bell rang. Mr. John worked him at the cotton gin but couldn't rest with Curtis around moving belts and pulleys. With time, Curtis gravitated to the livestock and found a niche.

Curtis caught the brunt of many jokes contrived by the field hands. Mr. John protected him before his death.

The barn gave Curtis refuge. He spent each day feeding, cleaning, petting, and talking to the animals. Mr. John chastised Curtis for over grooming the animals. He created bald spots on a prize Tennessee Walker's mane from the sheer amount he groomed the poor animal. Curtis loved animals and he told folks. Even the most understanding and even-tempered person found it trying; Bully possessed neither an even temper nor understanding.

———

When Bully stormed from the farm office, dust engulfed him. Doc Grasson's green Chevy came to a halt. Bully turned and started toward the far end of the equipment shed. Alice Fae broke into a sweat at the sight of Bully. Doc Grasson exited the truck and made his way toward the crippled Bully. Alice Fae ran into Miss Lillian's house.

"Bully, wait up!"

Bully slowed his crippled gait and turned. "Doc, not to be mean, but I'm not having a good day."

"Well, Bully, it's not your meanness concerning me. I don't want you to lose that foot. Sit down and let me see what's going on."

"It's been hurting like hell, Doc."

"Doc, if Ms. Lillian doesn't mind, I could ride back with you and take care of it now."

"Bully, that's a fine idea. Get in the truck."

When Doc Grasson pulled on the office doorknob, to alert Ms. Lillian about Bully's idea, Francina fell into his arms. He caught her and helped her regain her balance. Their eyes met. He tipped his hat. She blushed and went on her way.

Doc Grasson regained his composure and stuck his head into the office.

"I'll be taking Bully up to the house about that foot."

"If you haul him off, you better haul him back!"

"And another thing, I saw just what happen."

Their eyes locked. *Tic toc. Tic toc.* Mr. John's old clock permeated the silence.

Doc walked out. He and Bully got in the truck and proceeded to Doc Grasson's place.

Doc broke the silence.

"Bully, what has life been like without Mr. John around?"

"Well, I can't explain it. Do you know how one or two logs can cause a whole river of logs to get hung up?"

"Keep talking." Doc slowed for a pothole in the road.

"Like north is not north anymore?"

"Yeah, something like that."

"I felt like that when Olga died. Didn't want to get outta bed for the longest time. I started doing things out of character."

Doc thought of his morphine addiction.

"Yeah." Bully thought about his drinking.

"When are you going to tell me, what happened to that foot?"

"Doc, I shot it while I was cleaning my gun. I thought I told you already."

"Maybe you did."

Doc knew a gunshot wound when he saw one. This was no gunshot wound. The gravel clinked against the under carriage of Doc Grasson's truck.

"Bully, what happened to your mother, if you don't mind me asking?"

Bully did not entertain thoughts of his mother; it was far too painful.

"Doc, I don't know what happened to her. I have only heard stories of her. It's strange never to have met your mother. I always hoped she would appear one day, but she never did."

They fell silent. The Chevy made its way through the Mississippi countryside over dusty gravel roads.

They passed over the Mud Creek Bridge about five miles upstream from the fjord. They both flashed on the night Mr. John died. Doc Grasson and Bully kept silent.

Bully broke the silence. "Doc, can I ask you a question"

"Sure."

"Do you know who raped my mamma?"

Doc Grasson recoiled from the question.

"No, son. Some said a stranger raped her. The County Fair set up about that time. Some dogs are better left sleeping, Bully."

"It bothers me, but I don't talk much about it."

Three trucks and a team of mules pulling a wagon awaited the country doctor. Sick kids in their mother's arms and Joe Hill, who held his hand in a bloody diaper, waited on the porch. By the time Doc treated everyone and got a cast on Bully's foot, it was late afternoon.

Miss Lillian's old chime clock struck three. A faint knock tapped on the green screen door. Jessie appeared through the screen.

Miss Francina greeted him with a warm smile. Her hair blazed in the afternoon light of autumn. She wore a beautiful white blouse with a large cameo under her chin. Her pleated red skirt fell well below her knees.

Beautiful and Miss Francina were one to Jessie. His slicked down hair showed the imprint of his baseball cap, which he held in this hand. He stood dazed.

"Come in, Jessie. I've looked forward to our talk all day."

"Make sure his shoes are clean!" Miss Lillian called from the kitchen.

"He's fine, Mother," Miss Francina said.

She cut her eyes in her mother's direction.

"Let's sit at the piano."

They walked into the parlor and took a seat at the beautiful concert Grand Steinway. Jessie's heart raced. His mother had worked for Miss Lillian since his birth, but Jessie never entered through these doors. He often could hear Miss Francina play while he and his father worked down at the equipment shed. Miss Francina's gift; making everyone around her feel special. Jessie was no exception. He forgot his cuts and bruises and his busted lip. He forgot the wrath of his father the evening before. Inhaling Miss Francina's perfume, he lost himself in the moment.

"Miss Alice Fae said you might help me out?"

"Yes, ma'am," Jessie said.

"Well, I've been away to a wonderful school, and I've learned a lot about music. When I got home, I got to thinking about who in all the world would I like to share these new ideas and talents with. Do you know the one and only person who came to my mind?"

Jessie returned from his trance.

"No, ma'am,"

"You, Jessie."

She took her long index finger and touched his nose. She giggled and smiled.

Jessie levitated, floated up near the ceiling and floated back to earth at least in his mind.

"Jessie, would you like to learn to play the piano?"

"Yes, ma'am!"

Jessie's consequences for saying yes to piano lessons were far removed from the moment.

Alice Fae, always invisible, worked in the next room. She hung to each word muffled by the wall. She ironed, dusted, swept, cleaned; the adjoining room sparkled. She experienced excitement for Jessie, but there was fear. too.

Miss Francina introduced Jessie to his first piano instruction book and told him not to worry about his lack of a practice piano. She arranged with Miss Lillian, over her initial objections, for him to practice three days a week on the Steinway.

————

Darkness settled on another hot Mississippi autumn day. Doc Grasson dropped Bully off at the barn.

"Two things, Bully. You're going to be in that cast for at least six weeks, and don't get any water on my handy work, you hear me?"

"Yes, sir. And thanks for all you have done for me today, Doc."

"Not a problem, Bully. And when you are ready to tell me the real story about your foot, I'm ready to listen." Doc winked and climbed into his truck.

Bully watched Doc's green Chevy fade around the curve.

"Bully, I just love animals," Curtis said.

"I love animals, too. Curtis."

"But I really love animals, Bully."

"Okay Curtis, you really love animals. You win."

"Bully, I really, really love animals."

"Okay, goddamn it! You really, really love animals."

"Bully, I really..."

Bully put his hand over Curtis's mouth.

"Curtis, shut up or I'll... kill you." His lips pressed against his teeth.

Curtis's eyes bulged, and his face reddened. Seconds ticked by.

"Now, I'm going to take my hand off your mouth, and you are not going to say it. Right?"

Curtis nodded his head in the affirmative. Bully lifted his hand and Curtis's lips did not move. Bully's eyes dared him to utter a word. Curtis remained silent for twenty seconds: then thirty seconds. Bully's threat seemed to be working.

After a minute, Curtis whispered, "Bully, Miss Lillian says you've got to do what I say."

"Yeah, you're the boss, Curtis. I'm just a third-class peon and a slave to your every demand."

"Well, the first thing we got to do is haul three dead hogs off. They been laying back there in the stall for three days."

"What the hell are you talking about, Curtis?"

"One job we've got is hauling dead hogs off. With as many as we got, bound to be one or two dead every day."

"Curtis, I ain't hauling no dead hogs off."

"Miss Lillian said you have to do what I say, and I say we're hauling dead hogs off."

"Curtis, do you have to spit and get bug eyed every time you tell me what I've got to do? At least stand back!"

Bully stepped back.

"Okay, Curtis. It's getting late and I want to get home. Let's haul dead hogs off. Get the tractor and wagon."

"Miss Lillian won't let us use a tractor. We've got to use mules and a sled."

"Mules and a sled? Jesus!"

"Nothing wrong with mules, Bully. I love mules. And don't be rolling your eyes and shaking your head every time I say something," Curtis directed.

"I know I've arrived in Hell," Bully whispered and walked away.

Curtis went around behind the barn. After a few minutes, he returned. He stood in the back of a homemade sled fashioned from bridge timbers and pulled by two sorrel mules. He pulled up to Bully and motioned for him to get in. Bully hobbled over with his new cast and climbed in.

"This is a bad dream, God. You know that." Bully raised his hands toward the heavens.

"I'm staring into the ass of two mules and the eyes of one idiot!" Then the thought occurred: *This is better than staring into the ass of one idiot and the eyes of two mules.*

Curtis grinned. "I just love animals, Bully."

Bully shook his head, laughed, and surrendered. He knew defeat.

Curtis's mules made their way to Bully's house. Rover's barked,. No lights were on and Alice Fae's mamma's dresser still sat on the porch. Alice Fae and Jessie were not home.

"Whoa, mule!" Curtis brought the team to a halt.

Bully made his way off the sled. When he stepped off the platform, Rover rounded the corner of the sled and hit Bully in the chest.

"Damn it, Rover! Knock it off!"

Rover knocked him down, licked him in the face, and barked with excitement. Curtis laughed and cheered Rover on. Bully grabbed the side of the sled and pull himself up. Rover made wide circles in protest around the mule team.

"I just love dogs," Curtis said.

"Curtis, go home." Bully rolled his eyes and laughed.

"I'll pick you up in the morning, Bully. We are bound to have another dead hog or two."

"Damn, Curtis. You need to find out who's killing all them hogs. Or maybe they'll kill'um all and get it over with."

"Bully don't say that! I love hogs."

"I know. I know. You love hogs. See you tomorrow, Curtis. Now, go home."

Bully hobbled to the house. Curtis turned the mules around and drove away. Bully listened to Curtis talking to the mules. His voice faded.

Bully entered the cracked door and walked into the clutter: boxes were scattered, and what little furniture Bully and Alice Fae owned was in disarray. His childhood baseball glove protruded from a hole in a tattered box; it was the one Mr. John had given him years ago. Bully sighed and lifted the box with some effort. He unloaded the box in a back room along with Alice Fae's favorite dress—the one Mavis made for her on her eighteenth birthday. He moved some furniture around and even got Alice Fae's mamma's dresser off the porch. He pulled the dresser through the living room toward the bedroom.

Rover barked and focused on the driveway. Bully hobbled toward the front door and met Alice Fae and Jessie on the steps.

"Hey, sugar. Where you been?"

"Down at Mavis', Alice Fae stared at the floor.

"How's your buddy Mavis doing?"

"She's doing good, Bully. Bu... Bully, you don't remember about last night, do you?"

"What about last night?"

"Jessie, darling. Come here." Alice Fae reached out for Jessie.

Jessie made his way toward his mother.

"Mamma, it's all right, we don't have to talk about it."

"Talk about what?" Bully said.

Alice Fae turned Jessie around and lifted his shirt. Jessie grimaced when the material pulled away from the open wounds.

"Who did this!?"

"You did, Bully."

"No! No! Alice Fae are you out of your mind?! I would never do anything like that." Bully reached over and hugged Jessie.

"Bully, you did. You were drunk, but you did it last night. You don't remember, do you?"

"No, no." Bully's voice trailed off. He sank down into the nearest chair.

"It's all right, Daddy, you didn't mean to," Jessie said.

"I was scared to come home, Bully," Alice Fae said.

"Scared to come home? Alice Fae, I'm your husband."

"Not last night, Bully. I didn't know *that* person."

"Alice Fae, I don't know what to say. I know the last two or three weeks have been the worst time of my life; like a bad dream."

Bully turned to Jessie.

"Jessie, I'm sorry. Your daddy should never have done that. It won't ever happen again, Jessie. I promise. Please forgive me, both of you. You are all I've got."

Bully's voice trailed off. Jessie reached over and gave his father a hug. Alice Fae joined in. Rover stuck his nose in Bully's crotch.

———

Several days passed. Bully and Curtis fed, watered, and doctored livestock: and they hauled dead ones off. Miss Lillian transformed into a hellcat, making a huge push to get the crops out before winter. Jarvis, Cleo, and the field hands prayed for rain and relief from Miss Lillian. Jessie and Miss Francina made great progress on their music lessons.

Mr. Simmons, the school bus driver, spotted Rover a half mile from Jessie's house. Like clockwork, Rover hid under a group of plum bushes waiting for Jessie. When the bus passed, Rover gave chase toward Jessie's stop. Mr. Simmons flopped the old bridge bolt down, which he had fashioned into a lever for the red hand painted *Stop* sign. The brakes screeched, and the old converted milk truck came to a halt. Jessie departed the bus and greeted Rover. Doc Grasson's green Chevy pulled behind the bus. The old truck pulled away with a cacophony of screaming kids and a cloud of dust. Doc eased the Chevy alongside Jessie and Rover.

"Hi, Doc. Somebody sick?"

"No, Jessie. I was looking for you."

"Me? What for?"

"Let me ask you something."

"Long as it doesn't have anything to do with nasty tasting medicine or needles."

"No Jessie, nothing like that."

"Okay, go ahead." Jessie leaned into the truck window.

"Your mother said you like to read. Is that right.?"

"Yes, sir."

"I brought you a few books, if you're interested."

"What kind of books?"

"Civil War books."

"Oh, boy. Yes sir, I'm interested!"

Doc Grasson reached over and retrieved a box with several books. He handed them to Jessie.

"Look through these, Jessie. If you like them, I have plenty more."

"Gee, Doc, you sure are nice. Thanks." Jessie beamed with a warm smile.

"How did you bust your lip, Jessie?" Doc Grasson asked, forever the sleuth.

Jessie's smile faded. "Got into a fight at school," Jessie lied.

"I hope you got in a few licks yourself."

Jessie did not respond.

"Well, Jessie, I got to be moving up the road. Your daddy called me and wanted to know if I knew anything about sick hogs. I tell you, Jessie, don't be like me. You must learn to say No when you need to. I'll go by the barn and see if I can help. See you later, son." Doc's Chevy disappeared around the curve.

Jessie gave Rover his book satchel; a ritual. Jessie carried the box of books with his left arm while flipping through the pages of the top book with his right. When his boot hit the first rung on the steps to the porch, a drop of rain hit the worn brown leather. A broad grin appeared on Jessie's face. Rain meant no cotton picking. Rain meant playing with Rover. Rain meant reading Doc Grasson's books. Jessie placed the books on the bed and got down on his knees.

"Dear God, please let it rain. I won't play with my food. I'll take more baths. I won't talk in church if I go, and I'll quit calling Rebecca Smith a sow. Amen."

The sky opened and the most beautiful, slow rain fell. Jessie flipped backwards off the porch. He performed cartwheels. He and Rover spent all afternoon in the swing. Jessie read Doc Grasson's books and Rover slept. Jessie's life took a dramatic turn on this fall afternoon. From that porch swing, Jessie learned he could transport himself to another time. He devoured Doc Grasson's books. He learned names like Jackson, Mead, Longstreet, Burnside, Stuart, Grant, and Lee. He learned places like Antietam, Chancellorsville, Manassas, Shiloh, Fredericksburg, and Gettysburg. Jessie promised Doc Grasson a hug the next time he saw him.

SUMMONED

Bully's second week with Curtis started with a question.

"Bully, you ever heard of a blowout?" Curtis asked.

"Sure, our tractor tires have them all the time."

"No, Bully. I ain't talking about that kind of blowout. I'm talking about a hog blowout."

"Curtis, what the hell are you talking about? Hogs don't have blowouts."

"Got two back there in that pen and we've got to fix'um."

"Curtis, I don't want to ask, but I better. What's a hog blowout?"

"See Bully, hogs like to stay warm at night. It gets cold quick after the sun goes down, starting in the fall." Curtis's cadence slowed. His eyebrows furred. He pulled Bully closer.

"They get into piles of twenty to thirty." Curtis lowered his voice; he grew grave and solemn. "The ones in the middle stay warm. The ones on top sleep cold, and the ones on the bottom get blowouts from the weight of all the hogs on top of them."

"Curtis, I'm afraid to ask, but here goes: what the hell is a blowout?!"

"It's when a hog's guts blow out their butt."

"Jesus! Curtis, that's the most disgusting thing I ever heard!"

"Well, besides feeding and watering, we've got two dead hogs and two blowouts. Want to see one?"

"Not especially." Bully rolled his eyes and sighed.

"Well, we got to fix'um so, we might as well get to it."

Curtis led Bully past several stalls filled with assorted calves and goats, to a side shed that provided shelter for the hogs. When Bully and Curtis turned the corner, the word went through the herd it was feeding time. A stampede of two hundred hogs erupted toward the side shed. They squealed, shoved, bit, and rooted. Bully's thoughts ceased to function.

"Curtis!" Bully screamed over the porcine chaos. "We'll die if we go in there!"

"Got to feed 'um first! Settles them down! See, there's one," Curtis pointed to a two hundred-pound red Duroc hog in the corner. It wheeled around to get a better position in the feeding frenzy. When it turned, Bully saw about six inches of its intestines hanging from its end.

"Damn, Curtis, that terrible. How can we help him?" Bully's compassion and nausea battled.

"Got to feed them first.".

Curtis and Bully spent the next thirty minutes pouring shelled corn in long V-shaped oak troughs. The two placated the mass of hungry hogs. The squeals and shoves gave way to munching and chewing.

"I'll be right back!" Curtis said.

He disappeared around the corner. After several minutes, he returned with a three-foot length of garden hose.

"Curtis, now what are you doing?"

"Mr. John showed me how to fix a blowout. And I'm about to show you. If we don't fix it, the other hogs will kill the one with the blowout by chewing and pulling on its guts."

"What?"

Bully's thoughts drifted to the days of sunshine, the expansive fields, the roar of powerful tractors, and the camaraderie of the field hands. Curtis pulled his Case knife from a pocket and cut the hose into four-inch lengths.

"Now what, Curtis?" Bully's curiosity grew.

"The first thing is, you need a garden hose. I like the green ones. Then, we cut about this much off." Curtis cut another four inches off.

"Then we stick the short hose up the hog's butt."

"Jesus Christ, Curtis!" Bully pulled his red handkerchief from his back pocket and wiped the sweat from his brow.

"Don't say *we* when you're talking about sticking a garden hose up a pig's ass. And I don't care what color the damn hose is."

Curtis grinned.

"Bully don't butt in while I'm explaining what Mr. John taught me! Now, where was I? Oh, yes, the hose goes up the pig's butt. Then *we* take these." Curtis restated the plural with authority. He then pulled a handful of rubber bands from his bib pocket.

"We wrap the rubber band round and round the hose real tight. This squeezes the gut to the hose, cuts off the blood, and makes it fall off in about a week. The hose got to stick out a bit. Heck, Bully, a picture's better than a wagon load of words. Just watch this."

Curtis jumped over the fence and made his way to a big red Duroc. He eased behind the hog with great care. While it ate, Curtis, with the dexterity of a surgeon, performed the procedure. Bully watched in disbelief.

"Bully, you try one."

Bully felt queasy, but he didn't want to be outdone by Curtis, either.

He crawled over the fence and made his way out into the sea of hogs toward Curtis. Curtis extended his offering to Bully's trembling hand: a length of green hose and a rubber band.

"Dark one over there." Curtis pointed to a big Hampshire near the watering trough.

Bully made his way over to the hog. Curtis moved to the fence and crawled over, leaving Bully in the pen.

"Curtis, you tell anybody about this, and I'll shove this hose up your ass. I promise."

Curtis laughed.

Bully approached the rear of the hog. His hand trembled and his tongue dried. Bully took the hose and pushed it into the hog. The hose disappeared.

"Curtis, I've lost the hose. Bring me another one."

"Can't, Bully, you got to find it."

"Find it!? What are you talking about find it?"

"Find it, Bully. The hog might die if you don't find it. Feel for it with your fingers, Bully." Curtis smiled.

Bully probed the warm, bloody flesh with his fingers: over to the left, no; to the right, not there. Sweat dripped from Bully's nose onto the back of the hog. Bully's knees trembled. He looked up to see Curtis sitting on the fence, his teeth sunk into a *Moon* pie.

"Augh!" Bully wretched, losing his breakfast on top of the Hampshire. Curtis screamed out in laughter. Two hundred hogs exploded in a porcine wave. Bully's feet flew toward the havens, cast and all. Hogs carried Bully on their backs until he disappeared into the chaos. They knocked down a key support structure on the side shed. Timber and roofing pelted the hogs only to make matters worse. One corner of the shed collapsed. When the last hog escaped, Bully lay in a fetal position, covered in hog manure.

———

Bully trudged toward home. Cuts and bruises marinated in hog manure covered his body. Every orifice contained hog feces despite washing in the now familiar horse trough. Vulgar sound emanated from the wet shoe of his good foot.

The sun beat down. Bully's bad foot pounded. He heard the familiar sounds of a Farmall. Without turning his head, he knew Jarvis and Cleo were behind him. Eyes forward, dust engulfed Bully and gasoline fumes permeated his nostrils. Jarvis backed off the throttle and came to a stop.

"Mr. Bully, you look like you been on the wrong end of ugly." Jarvis grinned.

"Jarvis, I've been on the wrong end of a pig this morning."

"We'd give you a ride, but we got to get this cotton to the gin. That Miss Lillian be watching us like a hawk."

"That's OK, Jarvis. I don't want you and Cleo to get into trouble."

"Mr. Bully, when will you be getting back to the fields?"

"Cleo, your guess is good as mine. Miss Lillian's got me down at the barn with that idiot, Curtis, pushing water hoses up pig butts."

Cleo and Jarvis grinned.

"Mr. Bully, it's not the same with you and Mr. John gone. We seem to be just going thru the motions."

There was a slight shift in the breeze and Jarvis found himself downwind to Bully.

"Whew! There are a lot of things that smell round this farm, Mr. Bully, but right now, you be the worst! We got to be getting to the gin. Watch out for those hogs." Jarvis flashed his gold teeth, throttled up the Farmall, and pulled away.

Bully felt sad. He wanted to be on that Farmall. He wanted to be in the seat: a breeze hitting him in the face.

Bully, lost in thought, jumped when the blast of a truck horn brought him back to the present. He wheeled around on his good foot. Willard slipped behind Bully in the old Ford and his goofy grin appeared through the dirty windshield.

"Willard, you scared the living daylights outta me!"

"Man, you must have been on some other planet because I could have run you over and you would've never known. Shit, Bully, you smell God awful."

"Can you give me a lift down to my place? I had a bout with some hogs and lost this morning."

"Giving you a ride will put a strain on our friendship if I let you ride in the passenger seat. How's about you get in the back?"

"Do I smell that bad, Willard?"

"Bully, when you're in it, you can't smell it. I ain't in it, so I can smell it. I ain't getting in it, just so I can't smell it. Trust me, son, you flat out stink."

"I get it. The back it is."

Bully hobbled around and took the hooked chains from the tail gate and let it down, making a seat. He worked his way on to the tailgate and gave Willard a nod. The black Ford lurched forward. When the dust covered truck passed a clump of plum bushes, Rover jumped. He gave chase. Rover caught the Ford when Willard slowed to turn toward the "mansion." Rover landed in the back of the truck licking Bully in the face. Bully gave no resistance.

Bully cleaned up at the pump. Willard sat in the swing and

played with Rover. Bully made his way up the porch steps. Water dripped from his chin.

"Bully, why don't me and you go for a ride?"

"Willard, the last time I went on a ride with you, it cost me two days of my memory. Not to mention having nightmares of you and that chicken. No thanks."

"Bully, that was entertainment. This is a business trip."

"Business trip? What kind of business trip?"

"Mr. Carl wants to talk to you."

"Carl Butcher, that bootlegging crook you work for?"

"Now, Bully, don't be bad mouthing my boss, Mr. Carl. No, he ain't no saint, but the money's good."

"Why does he want to see me?"

"Mystery, to me. Let's go see."

"Well, I'll go, but I ain't the damn fool you are."

There were a handful of individuals who ran Lee County: Mr. C.C. Bates, the banker; Mr. P.H. McDonald, the cotton buyer; Mr. Goldberg, the editor; Buford King and Carl Butcher, rival bootleggers.

Bully and Willard loaded into the Ford and headed toward Guntown. Bully threatened Rover with his life if he followed. Rover pretended to listen. When the truck disappeared, Rover hit the cotton field behind the "mansion," running. Rover possessed impeccable timing. He could, via a shortcut, beat any land bound vehicle known to man, to his plum bushes.

When Willard found third gear on the old Ford, he turned to Bully.

"You might want to poke around under that seat."

Bully fumbled from the jack, to the lug wrench, to a paper sack. He pulled the sack out and found a quart of Wild Cat. Bully groaned, took a swallow, and passed it to Willard.

"That pretty good."

"My special blend. Old car batteries and one dead goat. Unique, huh?"

"Willard don't torture me with the details."

Rover stood in the road near the plum bushes when Willard and Bully rounded the curve in the road.

"That damn dog, I ought to kill him! Rover, git back to the house. Kick it, Willard. Go!"

Willard rammed the accelerator to the floor; gravel flew, and the dust rose. Rover chased the old Ford until a rabbit crossed his path.

Once past the taste, the whiskey felt warm and comforting to Bully. He settled back in the old Ford and felt the breeze on his face through the window vent. Willard drove in silence for several miles when a troubled look crossed his face.

"Bully, do you mind if I ask you a personal question?"

"Long as it doesn't have anything to do with fucking chickens."

"Nah, this is not like that. I'm puzzled by something. Here you are, the best damn tractor driver in these parts. Born on one. Me, they scare me. But you, you're a natural. Mr. John raised you on one. Now, here comes the troubling part. How come you had to be the one on that damn tractor when Mr. John died? Knowing how you felt about Mr. John and everything. Why not Jarvis? Cleo? Anybody but you. Mr. John could have been on it."

Bully remained silent. He took another drink of whiskey Bully stared at the faint blood trail from the chicken's head on the windshield. Tears welled in his eyes.

"Willard don't think I haven't asked myself that question a thousand times since Mr. John died. Why did I have to be in that seat? What could I have done different? Maybe I'm not as good as I thought I was. My thoughts are like a snake with its tail in his mouth. I keep coming back to the place I started. If it had wheels and rolled, I wanted to be in the seat. Begged for it. Would fight for it. Well, that night I got what I wanted. I owned the seat. The loneliest place in the world, that night, was that seat. The sick part is, I still want to get back on one. Crazy, huh?"

"Well, somebody has to drive. Can't everybody be in the wagon." Willard punched Bully on his good leg. "Ole buddy, if we were going down that slick as owl shit fjord at Mud Creek one more time, I'd want you driving. No doubt. No hesitation." Willard gave Bully a wink.

"Thanks, Willard. I need to hear words like that. The ones banging around in my head are a far cry from what you just said. My thoughts are vicious and dark. They are chopping my guts up. I don't know how to turn 'um off, either, except for this mule kicking stuff we're drinking. I've got to get back on a tractor soon or the doubt will eat me up, Willard. Kind of like getting back on a horse that bucked you off. Mr. John always said to 'die and go to Hell before you take a whipping.' Well, I got to get back in that seat or it's a whipping."

Bully bit into his lip.

———

Alice Fae enjoyed her morning walks to Miss Lillian's. The three miles gave her time to reflect, see the sunrise, and smell the freshness of a new day. Bully had been treating her better since the horrible night of the beating. She still awoke with nightmares. She tried to push the bad feelings away and lock them in the basement. But sometimes they rose through the flooring and moved over her. On those occasions, she felt nauseated and weak. Today, however, she felt stronger.

When Alice Fae approached Miss Lillian's, she heard the

old woman screaming from the road. She recoiled. Her good feelings faded. She grabbed her stomach. The familiar pain returned.

"You listen to me, you ole coot! I need that fuel out here by noon today. I am two weeks from getting this crop out, and no two-bit jerk like you is getting in my way. I don't give a damn about who died or who didn't. And another thing: the last time that idiot driver was out here, he ran over one of my pullets. You tell him he owes me a chicken, or his ass is mine. You got me straight?"

Alice Fae slipped in the back, careful not to slam the screen door. Miss Lillian replaced the earpiece in the cradle and smiled.

"Where in hell have you been? You on vacation or something?" Miss Lillian said. She grabbed the earpiece and turned the crank on the phone. "Rose, get me the cotton gin," she ordered the operator.

Alice Fae tried to get a word in, "But, Miss—"

"I don't have time to mess with you, Alice Fae. Just git that washing going and see if Francina needs you. Scat!"

"Yes, ma'am."

Alice Fae moved with haste toward the washing area and filled the tub with water. Before the water reached the first ring, Miss Lillian entered the back porch.

"That low life husband of yours walked off and left Curtis yesterday afternoon. I put him down there to help Curtis, and he can't even do that! You two are a match made in Heaven, I swear."

"But..."

"Don't but me, girl. You tell Bully he better steer clear of me or the bear might just get that other foot."

"But..."

"I told you not to 'but' me! Get that washing going, hang

the rugs, and beat the dust out you missed last time." Miss Lillian stormed off.

Those rugs got the beating of their life.

———

Carl Butcher's reputation grew daily as the meanest son of a bitch in Lee County. He worked hard and cultivated the image. He considered a negative comment a compliment. He also excelled at what he did: making and selling whiskey. You might say Carl provided a service. He delivered a product his customers desired. The Christians attempted to drive demand down, but human nature drove it up. Carl Butcher bet on human nature. The story goes, three big shots drove down from Memphis to cut a deal on entering his lucrative market. He killed them on his front porch and shot himself in the stomach with their gun to make it appear it was in self-defense. He walked. His chief adversaries were Buford King, a rival bootlegger, and Sheriff Bigelow. After many bloody battles, Carl and Buford settled on a loose arrangement. Carl took the north end of Lee County and Buford had the south. This worked while cash flow expanded, but during hard times, all bets were off. Sheriff Bigelow posed more of a nuisance during election years. He feared Carl Butcher and Buford King, with good reason.

Carl celebrated his 50th birthday, but the years of hard living extracted a toll. The most outstanding facial feature he possessed was a long scar beginning above his right ear and ending at the bottom of his round chin. Carl loved knives and found himself on the wrong end of one in a fight many years ago. His signature items were a toothpick protruding from the corner of his mouth and a .38 snub nose revolver hanging from a holster under his arm. He made no pretense to hide the fact. He possessed a loud voice and his mood was temperamental. Carl's most unsettling feature, however, was his unpredictability. He wrapped his arms around you in one moment and twisted a knife in you the next. Some called him a viper.

Federal agents ambushed and killed his father when Carl turned two, and his mother died of exhaustion and worry trying to raise seven children on a cleaning woman's pay. Authorities separated Carl from his brothers and sisters and placed him in an orphanage at the age of ten. He grew defiant and the seeds of his bitterness festered.

Carl operated a combination service station and dry goods store in Guntown, which served as a front for his real business: whiskey. He employed a cadre of young men he called *his boys. Carl's boys* owned a common trait: they were sick of picking cotton and willing to do anything to escape the fields.

Willard fit that description.

A steady stream of cars moved in and out of Carl's place, day and night. A large field of corn grew behind the store. Rumors flew that his boys would bury half pint bottles of whiskey under designated corn plants to avoid confiscation of the inventory.

Bully's watch showed two o'clock when they drove under the shade tree at Carl's place. Bully's curiosity and good judgement were battling it out. He hobbled from the old Ford. Over the porch, a large sign hung with Carl's name in big red letters. Two old church pews, once painted green, were on the front porch. Four cats crouched under the pews attempting to stay cool. Two gas pumps and a red kerosene dispenser were the most prominent items making up the store facade. Tools to repair truck flats lay scattered across the porch floor. Willard and Bully walked in the front door. Bully noticed dust on the shelf items. *If it wasn't liquid, it didn't move,* Bully thought. The wooden floors creaked, and the old paddle fans struggled to stay even with the heat. They walked back to a large pot belly stove in the rear. A white man played a game of chess with a small wiry black man.

The white man spoke,

"You boys come on in." He got up from his game and approached Willard and Bully. He extended his hand to Bully with a smile.

"Hi, son. My name is Carl Butcher. I was a close friend of Mr. John's. Mizel, get these boys a soda."

Carl seemed friendly, but it was the kind of friendly you couldn't trust. Mizel jumped up and moved toward the drink box.

"Root beer or RCs, gentlemen?"

"We'll take root beer," Willard spoke.

He knew Bully loved the sassafras drink.

Mizel popped the tops off two drinks and brought them over to the circle of cane bottom chairs sitting around the cold stove. Bully noticed ashes from last year's fires were still under the stove.

"Mizel, why don't you and Willard go for a little walk. I would like a little privacy." Mizel motioned toward Willard and pointed to the back door. Mizel enjoyed his role as Carl's right hand man. Bully's eyes darted toward Willard, and his heart moved to his throat. Willard shrugged his shoulders and flashed that goofy grin. Bully shuddered when the door slammed behind Willard and Mizel.

The ceiling fans attempted to break the gut-wrenching silence with little effect.

"Do you play the Royal game, son?" Carl looked down at the chess board.

"No, sir. Willard tried to teach me, but I could never sit still long enough."

"Those sixty-four squares can produce every emotion known to man. They become a world that is finite and manageable on the one hand, yet complex and beautiful on the other. I've seen greed, fear, ambivalence, and joy gallop across those 64 squares. You can tell a lot about a man by the way he handles himself over that board. I've seen hardened men pout and spineless babies become absolute killers on that board. I learned to play in the brig, before they kicked me out of the Navy. I got pretty good."

Carl seemed unbeatable to his "boys." He challenged them with an offer: a thousand dollars to any man who could beat him. Carl never lost.

He reached over and tipped the white king on its side.

"A hell of a man went down when Mr. John died. I feel bad for him. All the scum in the world and I hear Mr. John is dead. Makes me sick."

"No worse than I do, Mr. Carl."

"Look, son. I hear you've been taking it hard. I want to say, for one, I do not hold you responsible for Mr. John's death. He died doing what he enjoyed. Every man should be so lucky."

"Thanks, Mr. Carl."

"I also heard you gave those hypocrites, son of a bitches Hell over at Mt. Zion Church. You warmed my heart that day."

Carl gave out a belly laugh.

"I'm not proud of my actions, sir. As a matter of fact, I don't even remember that day."

"Well, I do and will for a long time."

Carl leaned toward Bully and a solemn expression moved across his face.

"Son, Mr. John and I talked many times about what would happen to our land if the other died. We both agreed the farms needed to be joined—informally, of course. Son, I aim to own that land, and I would like you to help me get it."

"What are you talking about, Mr. Carl?! I can't even get into the fields, since Miss Lillian took over."

"I understand she has not treated you well since Mr. John's death.

"That's putting it mildly, Mr. Carl."

"That old lady cannot afford one bad crop after pissing C.C. Bates off like she did."

Carl possessed an incredible information gathering network across Lee County. It was a powerful tool in the hands of a man with his abilities.

"I want you to help me give Miss Lillian a failed crop for next year. My plan cannot fail. I'll cut you in."

Bully jumped out of his chair. He thought, *Carl's lying. Mr. John would not do such a thing.*

"Thanks for the soda, Mr. Carl. I think you're talking to the wrong man. I have my differences with Miss Lillian, but Mr. John worked his whole life to put that land together, and I don't plan on being a part of destroying it. I'll be leaving, now."

Carl didn't flinch. This was just the opening move. He would win. Carl Butcher always won.

"Well, son, don't be foolish. I would make it very lucrative for you. Besides, with a wife and a young kid, a man like yourself needs to guard against unexpected misfortunes that present themselves from time to time."

Bully didn't miss the hidden threat in Carl's statement.

"You think it over. Mizel! Get Willard, and tell him to give this boy, here, a ride home."

Carl's lips pressed on his words.

GOOD DAYS & BAD DAYS

Jessie, lost in the rich past of the Civil War, finished reading Doc Grasson's books, *The life of Johnny Reb* and *The life of Billy Yank,* by Bell Irwin Wiley. Jessie became vigilant each afternoon hoping to see Doc's green Chevy. Two weeks passed when one afternoon, his truck appeared like a mirage from behind the school bus. He pulled into the drive. Rover climbed into the back of the truck.

"Hey, young man! Read any good books?"

"Doc Grasson, thank you, thank you! I read 'um all. Got any more?"

"Not a problem. I told you there were more where those came from. Listen, I was at Miss Lillian's place earlier today and ran into your mamma. I ask her about you and me taking a little ride up to Brice's Cross Roads. She said it would be fine if I could get Miss Lillian to release you from that cotton field prison."

Jessie's eyes froze on the old country doctor.

"Well, let me tell you. Miss Lillian challenged my every word, but I softened her up with a mess of turnip greens before I brought up the subject. She reckoned the cotton harvest hung in the balance of weather and hired help, not the efforts of a 12-year-old boy for one afternoon."

"Eureka! You're wonderful, Doc Grasson! Can we bring Rover?"

"Could we stop him from coming if we wanted to?"

Doc put the Chevy in reverse and backed into the road and headed for the Battlefield at Brice's Cross Roads. Jessie grinned. Rover reached around the cab of the truck and licked Doc Grasson through the window.

———

The silence between Willard and Bully cut deep, overshadowed only by the drone of the old Ford's engine. Five miles from Carl's, Bully exploded.

"You son of a bitch, you set me up! I thought you and me were friends. Friends, hah! You're just a paid whore for a snake in the grass bootlegger!"

"What the hell are you talking about, Bully? It's me, Willard, your running buddy!"

"Running buddy, my ass! You knew what Carl Butcher had in mind! Business? Yea, I got a little business trip from him!"

Willard pulled the truck over to the side of the road and came to a stop.

"Bully, what went on back there? I don't have a clue what you're talking about."

"You didn't know Carl Butcher has his eyes on Mr. John's land? You didn't know Carl wanted me to betray Miss Lillian? You didn't know Carl threatened me and my family with our lives if I didn't play his little game?"

"Bully, I swear on my mamma's grave. I'm not in on Mr. Carl's scheme."

"Willard, if you're lying, I will kill you."

"Bully, I'm shooting straight. You believe me?"

Bully looked straight ahead. Willard leaned toward Bully trying to think of something else to say.

"Willard, I want to believe you." Bully's voice took on a more rational tone. "Carl's boys don't have the best reputation in town, you know."

"Bully, I'm not proud of working for Mr. Carl. It's just easier to get in than to get out."

"I can't tell you what to do, screwed up as I am." Bully broke into a smile. "Yeah, I believe you." Bully reached over and tapped Willard's chin.

"Bully let's go over on the Tallahatchie River and see what's going on. I'm not ready to go home."

"Suits me, I'm not ready to go home either."

Willard put the Ford into low gear and pulled away.

Bully passed him the Wild Cat.

————

Jessie, excited about the prospects of spending an afternoon with Doc Grasson, fought to sit still. He tried to sit up straight in the truck seat like Doc Grasson. He tried to rest his arm on the truck window like Doc Grasson. He tried to sit big. Jessie felt important and special. His mind raced.

What would that sow Rebecca Smith, I mean, girl, think if she could see me with Doc Grasson? She's picking cotton and I'm headed for Brice's Cross Roads. Wait till I tell Miss Francina. Bet Jarvis and Cleo are wondering what happen to me. I can't wait to tell Mamma and Daddy. Jessie's galloping thoughts stilled when Doc Grasson's Chevy came to a stop. Rover hit the ground chasing a butterfly. Jessie and Doc Grasson exited the truck.

"Now, Jessie, I want you to picture what I'm about to tell

you." Doc stood on a ridge overlooking a valley. He pointed to the west.

"Imagine seeing eight thousand plus Federal troops coming at you. That's what the Johnny Rebs saw on the morning of June 10, 1861. A fellow named General Sturgis commanded the Federal troops out of Memphis. It was a sight to behold. I can imagine the sounds of mules, wagons, and men making their way through this valley on that morning. Sun coming up over that ridge, shining in their eyes. Sturgis had some help. A fellow name Grierson was his right-hand man. Then he had officers with names like Winslow, Waring, Wilkins, Hoge, Bouton, and McMillian. Jessie, it was an unforgettable sight for the southern boys. Some of them were not much older than you."

Jessie could almost see the Federal troops on the horizon.

"If eight thousand soldiers were not enough, Sturgis had two hundred and fifty wagons with enough supplies to last twenty days. There were twenty-five ambulances. Those Federal boys brought artillery with them, too, about twenty cannons. Those Yankees were looking for a fight. Well, they didn't have long to wait. See, the Rebs had this fellow by the name of Forrest—General Nathan Bedford Forrest. Now, he was something. He was a cavalry officer."

Doc's voice was slow and steady.

"Jessie, when you hear the word *cavalry*, you want to think of men on horses. The cavalry is the eyes and ears of the infantry. This fellah Sturgis was a sharp general, I reckon, but, Forrest—well, he was a little quicker."

Jessie's mouth gaped and his eyes riveted on the old southern doctor. Doc Grasson sat on the running board. He picked up a stick and drew lines and formations in the dirt. Jessie looked at Doc's diagrams and formations, then he looked at the battlefield. He visualized that morning and his heart raced. Doc's descriptions of the battle on June 10, 1861, came to life.

"See, Jessie, timing is everything in life—was then, is now. Well, Forrest could have ridden down there and met the enemy and gotten in the middle of them. Forrest didn't do that. He waited. See that hill over there?" Doc pointed to a knoll covered with scrub oak.

"Yes, sir."

Jessie could almost hear the Rebs in the scrub oak, which were a beautiful golden orange color.

"In 1861, this whole area was covered with scrub oak, just like what you see there. The only area that was clear was the road Sturgis and his men traveled. This was a pig trail of a road; very narrow. Well, Forrest placed his cavalry in the bush and waited. Then, he waited some more.

"The tension between the advancing Federal forces and the waiting Confederate soldiers created too much excitement."

"What happened next, Doc Grasson?"

"See that creek yonder?" Doc pointed to a small stream running though the valley.

"There was a bridge on that creek. Just wide enough for one wagon at a time. Forrest, being a little quicker than Sturgis, waited."

"Doc Grasson, please don't start that waiting, again!"

"Well, in fact, Forrest *did* wait. He waited until Sturgis's eight thousand plus infantry crossed that nothing of a bridge, then he waited until all two hundred and fifty wagons and twenty-five ambulances crossed. His men were anxious, too, Jessie, but they were also disciplined. If Gen. Forrest said wait, they waited. When the waiting ended, it ended with a vengeance, Jessie. Forrest opened up on Sturgis's men with all he could muster: cannons; muskets; revolvers; and sabers. Confusion and panic broke out in the ranks of the boys in blue. The Yanks' day got off to a bad start; those Rebs came from all directions with that blood curdling scream, called the rebel yell. Those scrub oaks crawled with Johnny Rebs. The infantry fell back due to the ferocious fire from Forrest's men. Problem was, they didn't have much of a place to run. The wagons blocked the path. Then the teams and wagons tried to turn around. A wagon turned over on the bridge blocking the entire road. Mangled wagons, supplies, and men backed up against the bridge. For the Rebs, it was target practice. Forrest's boys were outnumbered two to one, but on that day, the morning of June 10, 1861, Gen. Forrest's boys gave the Yanks a licking."

Time stopped for Jessie while Doc Grasson related the story of Brice's Cross Roads. For a brief suspended moment, he felt transported to that fateful morning almost a hundred years ago. He heard the blasts, the horses, the smell of gun powder and the cries of men. He forever captured the allure of the distant past and his soul ached to know what Doc Grasson knew. There was no fear of being beaten. The only screaming was the battle cry of the rebel yell. There were no cotton fields. There was no worrying about his mamma. For Jessie, something magic happened on that hill overlooking the fields known as Brice's Cross Roads. The birds of passion and freedom had flown into his heart.

"Jessie! Jessie! Are you all right?" Doc broke into Jessie's moment.

"Yes, sir. Yes, sir." Jessie emerged from his daze.

"You know what I've often thought about?" Doc asked Jessie.

"What?"

"I've often thought it would be fun to get down in that old

creek bed and poke around sometime. No telling what we might find. You interested?"

"Yes, sir! Doc Grasson, that would be great. Let's do it now!"

"No, not today. Anything we might find will still be there later."

Doc walked over to the truck, opened the door and reached under the seat. He pulled out an elongated object wrapped in an old quilt.

"Jessie, I've been thinking about it, and I want to give you something."

He lay the blanket on the ground and unfolded it with great care. Jessie's heart raced with anticipation. Before Jessie's eyes appeared a .58 Cal. Springfield musket, ammo belt and canteen.

"My daddy gave them to me. You want them?" Doc asked.

"Do I want them?! Yes!"

"Like I said, my daddy gave them to me, and I'm not getting any younger. So, I figured you might take care of them for me. What ya say?"

"Doc, this is the happiest day of my life. Thank you! Thank you!"

Jessie gave the old country doctor a hug.

"Well, I best be getting you back home. Call old Rover and let's head back."

Jessie called out several times for Rover without success.

"Watch this," Doc Grasson said. He started the Chevy engine with a roar. Rover came running and jumped into the back of the truck. Doc Grasson winked at Jessie. Jessie smiled.

———

The Tallahatchie River winds through Mississippi like a snake. Most of the time, she's a peaceful home to raccoons, possums, foxes, an occasional bobcat and man. During heavy rains, the Tallahatchie becomes vicious. Her muddy waters invade towns, fields, homes, and becomes unforgiving. She was sleepy on this afternoon.

Willard pulled the old Ford under a huge oak overlooking the Tallahatchie and disconnected two wires. The engine died.

"Wow! Look at the ole girl, just as friendly as she can be, Willard said. But, let me tell you, that bitch can bite. Me and this other fool went looking for trouble one morning back in the Spring. He traded his brother-in-law a railroad jack for some sort of little old boat. He said it was like what the Indians used to have." Willard was drunk.

"Anyway, we came over here and put that lil' old boat in right down there. Willard pointed. Strange thing, though. On Sundays, people crawled this place except on this Sunday. That struck me funny, but we plowed on like idiots and put that boat in the water. Blind leading the blind, I reckon."

Bully grinned at Willard and sipped on the Wild Cat. He had heard this story twice, but Willard liked to tell it and Bully didn't mind.

"We hadn't gone a half mile when I heard this roaring sound. My heart jumped into my throat and sweat broke out all over me. We edged over to the bank and climbed this little bluff. Biggest goddamn waterfall you ever seen. Sleepy ole girl was in an ill mood that day. Well, here is where our senses left us. I wouldn't blink, and that fool I was with didn't blink, so the only thing left to do was to go over that fall. We figured. We connived. And we plotted against this ole gal. We figured two fellas smart as we were could out do any lil' ole fall that this sissy Tallahatchie could throw at us."

Willard got louder and louder.

"Well, we figured our strategy out to the letter. Dotted every i and crossed every t. Picked the perfect spot. Estimated the correct speed. Secured the supplies and gear. Got back in that boat and shoved off. We came in at the exact angle. Hit that spot perfect. That bitch swallowed us up. Whoosh! Water in the boat. Whoosh! More water in the boat."

Willard waved his arms around hitting the top of the truck cab and making high water sounds.

"Whoosh! Next thing I know, I'm tossed around under the water like I'm in one of those fancy ringer washing machines. I'm scratching, clawing, and digging, trying to get to the top. My mind's a racing. I'm thinking, I'm gonna be a mile down this ole river when I come up. Well, I came up and there was that damn waterfall staring me right in the face. I took a half a breath and got sucked right back under. Whoosh! That Tallahatchie gal humbled me. A sober thought hit me: *Willard boy, you're gonna die.*"

Willard had sucked Bully into the story, again.

"The strangest thing happened while I was under there. A calm passed over me like I'd never had before. I stared into the face of God or something. A conversation I heard between two ole river rats more than two years ago popped in my head. They were talking 'bout getting sucked under and stuff. They said to swim to the bottom. I remembered, even though I was drunk. Swim to the bottom. So, I stepped out on blind faith and did it. That ornery ole Tallahatchie spit me out like lukewarm drinking water. I gasped, wheezed, and coughed. When I came to the top. I was naked, except for my daddy's ring."

Willard held up his prized turquoise and silver ring.

"I grabbed a tree bent downstream from the current and

held on for dear life. I looked back at the fall and could see our little ole boat bobbing up and down like a cork. That angry bitch ate our boat. My buddy got flung over the fall like a rock in a slingshot. He made it to the bank. After I gathered myself, I swam in his direction. I pulled myself out and lay flat on my back for the longest time. My heart raced. I was water-logged and thankful to be alive. I never will forget the ride home. Life exploded around me. Colors were brilliant, smells washed over me, and I was alive. Every breath is a gift from God. Sometimes, I wish I could live in that moment. Hell, I wish I could get back there. It made me not take things for granted and not sweat the little stuff, Bully."

"That sure is a good story, Willard. I thought I was in that boat with you for a moment."

Bully passed Willard the Wild Cat.

"I'm sure glad the ole girl let you go, Willard." A moment connected the two. They fell silent.

"Bully, let's get out, stretch our legs and skip a few rocks across the water."

Willard and Bully made their way down the riverbank Willard ran and Bully hobbled. Willard ran toward Bully with a fishing reel he found on the bank. They practiced casting and rock skipping till their whiskey depleted energy dissipated. Willard helped Bully up the bank and suggested Jessie might like the fishing reel. They made their way back to the old Ford and climbed in. Willard tied the two wires together and hit the starter. The Ford came to life. The sun set on the Tallahatchie. Willard and Bully headed for Lee County and home.

———

Francina awoke to her mother's screaming and yelling at Alice

Fae. Miss Lillian's claim of being "high strung" proved correct, during times of duress. However, Francina felt for Alice Fae. Since returning from Europe, Francina loathed her mother's outbursts and felt protective of her. Alice Fae seemed to have no protective barrier between herself and the world and Miss Lillian made up a large part of her world. Each incident became a frontal assault with Alice Fae wilting under the fire, but Miss Lillian had no tolerance for weakness in herself or in others. She wanted to change it or kill it.

Francina waited until Alice Fae disappeared around the curve to ask her mother to join her in the parlor.

"Mother, may I talk to you concerning something that is bothering me very much?" Francina expressed firmness in her voice.

"Sure, dear. I don't have a lot of time. Jarvis and Cleo are expecting me to meet them at the cotton gin before dark."

"Mother," Francina chose her words with caution, "why do you treat Alice Fae so bad?"

"What do you mean, Francina? Get to the point."

"I feel so sorry for Alice Fae. I wish you would treat her better."

Miss Lillian sat on the edge of her seat. "Francina, Alice Fae is nothing but white trash. She has always been white trash, and she will die white trash. Her husband is white trash and that snotty nose kid of her's is white trash. You have more to concern yourself with than to be fretting over the likes of Alice Fae."

"Mamma, you treat Killer better than you treat Alice Fae."

"Killer's got more sense than Alice Fae."

"Mother be kind," Francina chastised her mother.

"Look, Francina, you need to be concerning yourself with meeting a nice boy, getting married, and having babies. Not fretting over the likes of simple-minded white trash like Alice Fae."

"Mother, what young man would risk getting past you and Killer to court me?"

"Francina, you are the prettiest girl in Lee County. Men will be lining up at the door soon as word spreads of your return from Europe. Now, I've got to go, Francina. You work at staying pretty and let me handle the black and white trash on this farm."

Miss Lillian rose, kissed Francina on the cheek and rushed out.

———

Darkness pervaded the Mississippi landscape. Bully and Willard made their way home. The Wild Cat worked, and the old Ford droned. Willard turned into Bully's drive. He hit the mailbox. It went flying but neither Bully or Willard noticed. Bully opened the door and fell on the ground. Rover pounced. He licked Bully's face and pulled on his shirt. Willard laughed, tossed the rod and reel onto the ground and circled the house with the Ford's accelerator to the floor. He got sideways near the south corner of Bully's house and hit Alice Fae's clothesline. Sheets went flying and the hens in the coop started squawking. Willard hit second gear when the Ford rounded the house. Rover released Bully and hit the cotton patch behind the house, running. He raced the old Ford to the plum bushes. Bully heard Willard screaming and yelling. Tail lights faded around the curve.

Bully never saw Willard again.

———

Alice Fae and Jessie arrived home an hour earlier. Doc Grasson and Jessie gave Alice Fae a ride home when they met her walking home from Miss Lillian's. During the preparations for supper, Jessie related his afternoon with Doc Grasson to his mother. His mouth ran with no hint of a pause to breathe. Alice Fae enjoyed his excitement.

The sound of the Willard's Ford crashing into the mailbox interrupted supper preparations. Alice Fae knew Willard and Bully were drunk. She ran to the churn and confiscated Bully's supply of Wild Cat and hid it behind the flour in the pantry. She ran for the window. Alice Fae and Jessie pressed their faces to the glass. Willard circled the house in wild commotion and headed home.

"Jessie, darling, don't say or do anything to upset your daddy! Promise."

Her heart raced, and her hands were sweaty. Bully staggered onto the porch with the fishing rod and made his way into the house.

"What are you looking at, woman?"

"You hungry, Bully?"

"Yea, I'm hungry. What's for supper?" Bully slurred.

"Black eyed peas, fried okra, cornbread, and fresh tomatoes."

"Sounds good to me. Jessie, come here. Look what Willard and I found down at the river."

Bully pulled the fishing rod from behind his back. Jessie's eyes lit up. Bully handed the fishing rod to Jessie who ran out to the front yard and attempted to cast without success. Alice Fae finished the supper preparations and called Jessie in for supper. The three sat down to eat. Jessie overflowed with excitement.

"Dad let's go fishing tomorrow. With that rod and reel, I bet we could catch the biggest fish in the world!"

Bully remained silent. He shoveled food into his mouth. His eyes were fixed on his plate. Jessie's excitement erupted to greater and greater heights fueled by the visions of big fish and time with his father.

"Eat your supper, Jessie." Alice Fae cut her eyes toward Jessie. Splotches appeared across her chest. Fork and knife were clinking on Bully's plate. Jessie's voice continued to rise with excitement. Alice Fae's eyes darted back and forth. She attempted to kick Jessie under the table.

Without warning, Bully backhanded Jessie across the face, knocking him into the living room area.

"Shut the hell up, boy." Bully's eyes locked onto Jessie's sprawled body lying on the wide plank oak floor.

Bully stood up and flipped the table into the air. Bowls, tea glasses, and food went flying. Bully lunged at Jessie. Alice Fae threw her body between the raging Bully and the terrified child.

"Bully, please don't! Please don't do this!"

"Get outta my way, Alice Fae! That little bastard is gonna learn a lesson tonight!"

"No! No! Bully please. Jessie, go to your room and don't come out! Alice Fae ordered Jessie, who scrambled off the floor and ran to the back room.

Bully scanned the room in a staggering stupor, looking for a target for his rage. He stumbled over to the churn and reached for his private supply of Wild Cat.

"Woman, where's my whiskey?"

"Bully, you don't need more whiskey."

"Don't' tell me what I need, woman!"

Bully staggered to the rod and reel. He picked it up and raised it over his head.

"Alice Fae, where's my goddamn whiskey."

"Bully, you don't need..."

Wham! Bully struck Alice Fae across the chest with the rod and reel.

"Where's my goddamn whiskey, Alice Fae?"

Wham! Once again Bully struck Alice Fae in the back when she turned, trying to get up from the first vicious blow. She went down again. She stayed down. Bully staggered to Jessie's door. He kicked it in. The door exploded in wood splinters. Bully staggered into the room.

"Where's my whiskey, you little shit?" Bully scanned the room.

Jessie did not respond. Bully jerked the closet door open and ripped the clothes down from the hangers. No Jessie. He looked under the bed. No Jessie.

"Jessie, you best be coming to me when I call you. You know what your mamma got for messing with me."

Silence.

Bully stumbled back into the living room and Alice Fae had disappeared. Bully made his way out to the front porch.

"Alice Fae! Jessie! You better get back in here!" The autumn Mississippi night offered Bully only whip-o-wills, crickets, and bull frog sounds. Lighting bugs dotted the darkness. He staggered back into the house and passed out on the couch.

CHECKMATE

Willard's Ford threatened to come apart. He rounded the curve and blew past the plum bushes. Rover waited. Willard struggled to see through the dirty windshield. He caught the glimpse of an old red truck sitting crossways in the road. Four men, with flashlights and shotguns, stood in front of the truck. Willard slammed on his brakes and went into a slide. Willard's Ford missed the truck but did not miss the high bank next to the blockade. It went high onto the bank and rolled over and over, plowing through a barbed wire fence and cutting a swath through a blackberry patch. The truck came to rest upside down in the back water of a small cattle pond. Willard crawled out the back window It's glass a victim of the first roll..

"That's a hell of a place to park a truck, fellas!" Willard muttered wiping mud from his face.

The four men approached Willard with flashlights and shotguns. It was Mizel and three of Carl's boys.

"Don't kill him. Boys. Mr. Carl wants him alive."

"Goddamn, Mizel! Is that the best place you can find to park that truck?"

Willard staggered out of the water. Carl's boys stuck shotguns in Willard's face and ordered him out onto the road.

"What you boys up to, Mizel? Watch those guns. Might hurt someone if you're not careful."

"Fellas, put this drunk in the truck and let's get outta here."

"Where we going, boys? Looks like for a little ride. What about my truck?"

"You're not going to need that truck where you're going," Mizel said.

Willard followed Mizel and Carl's boys to their truck. They threw Willard into the back and joined him with their shotguns. Mizel got behind the wheel and drove toward Guntown.

———

"Oh, Lord! Darling, I think I'm having me a religious experience! Don't stop! Don't stop!"

Mavis' legs pointed toward the ceiling. Dalton's eyes rolled into the back of his head. His nostrils flared. The headboard banged against the wall. The bed springs sang.

Bang! Bang! Bang! The screen door on the old house broke through Dalton's testosterone storm and Mavis crash landed back in Mississippi from her orgasmic flight.

It was Alice Fae.

"Mavis! Mavis! Let me in!"

Bang! Bang! Bang!

"Quick! Let me in!"

Dalton cussed, and Mavis grabbed for her panties. Mavis pulled herself together, knees weak, and made her way to the front door. Alice Fae rushed inside the house the moment Mavis unlocked the latch.

"Mavis! Mavis! Bully's done beat up on Jessie and me, again! Bully's done hurt Jessie; I know it! I know it!"

"Alice Fae, calm down, dear. Calm down." Mavis hugged Alice Fae. Mavis felt a warm wetness on Alice Fae's back. She lifted her hand toward the light and blood covered her hand.

"That does it! Dalton, come in here." Dalton came in with hair sticking straight up, bib overalls latched on one side, no shirt or shoes.

"Look, Dalton!" Mavis showed Dalton her hand.

"That son of a bitch Bully did this to Alice Fae!"

Dalton reached for his boots, lantern, and shotgun. Mavis ran for bandage materials.

"Don't kill him, Dalton! Don't kill him," Alice Fae pleaded with Dalton. "Just get Jessie and bring him here!"

"Dalton don't kill him, but don't let him know you're not," Mavis said. She spoke through gritted teeth.

———

Mizel and the boys rolled into Carl's place. Willard passed out during the ride. One of Carl's boys revived Willard with a bucket of water.

Mizel sold whiskey, but he hated drunks. Mizel surveyed the scene. No customers were in sight. Carl's boys drug Willard from the truck and man handled him toward the back door of Carl's place. Mizel reported to Mr. Carl. Carl instructed Mizel to lock Willard in a back shed and let him sleep off the whiskey. He wanted to see Willard the following day around two in the afternoon.

———

Dalton lived two miles from Bully's place. He walked at a brisk pace with the lantern off. A full moon made visibility manageable. Dalton's quick pace brought the light of Bully's place into view. He walked down the drive toward the house.

A single light illuminated the kitchen. Dalton approached the house.

"Bully, you in there? It's me, Dalton. Hey, Bully! Anybody home?"

Dalton cocked the shotgun. He walked up the steps onto the porch and looked in the open front door. There Bully lay, passed out on the couch. Scattered food and dishes covered the floor.

"Jessie, it's me, Dalton."

Nothing. Dalton entered the front door and made his way to the bedrooms. He raised the wick on the lantern, casting a dim light into the small rooms.

"Jessie! It's me, Dalton. Can you hear me?"

Rover bounded into the house and barked with great enthusiasm.

Dalton's heart stopped for a moment. Bully never moved. Dalton composed himself and stuck out his hand. Rover came over and licked Dalton's hand. He knew Dalton.

"Rover find Jessie for me. Go find Jessie."

Rover wagged his tail and barked. He went through the house, sniffing and looking. He bolted outside and circled the house. Rover raced down to the chicken coop. Rover barked and scratched at the chicken coop door. Dalton approached the coop and shined his lantern over into the coop. There Jessie sat, huddled in a corner, rocking back and forth, with his Civil War books. Dalton heard Jessie repeating a singsong chant while he rocked. Dalton interrupted Jessie.

"Hey, Jessie, it's me, Dalton."

"Who goes there, Yanks or Rebs?" Jessie emerged from his trance and spoke with authority.

"Well, Jessie, Rebs of course. Are you, all right? Your mamma's worried sick. She sent me to git you."

"Sir, I'm sure many mothers worry about their sons, but I'm lost from my detachment and must return to Major Pelham."

"Major who? Jessie, you're not making no sense."

"Major John Pelham, sir. I serve with Major John Pelham. We are part of Gen. J.E.B. Stewart's horse artillery. You mean you never heard of Major John Pelham, sir?"

"Jessie, I can't say I have. Let's you and me git on down to the house. Your mamma's worried sick."

"Sir, I need supplies and I need a horse. We are fighting for the Glorious Rebel Cause. Major Pelham would be pleased if you assisted me."

Dalton appeared confused and frustrated. "Jessie, damn it, if you will come with me, I'll help you get supplies."

"Very well, sir." Jessie collected his books and moved toward the lantern.

"That's a nice dog you got there, sir. Does he have a name?"

"Does he have a name?! Jessie, that's Rover!"

Dalton's frustration turned to anger when Jessie approached the light. Blood covered the right side of his face; his eye was swollen shut.

"Sir, with all due respect, why do you keep calling me, Jessie?"

"Darn it, Jessie, because that's your name. Now, let's quit jawing and get down to the house and get you cleaned up."

"Sir, my name is Private John Starke, serving under Major John Pelham, Chief Artillery Officer for General Jeb Stewart, Confederate States of America."

Dalton blurted out, "Whatever! Come on, soldier."

Dalton, Rover, and the young boy soldier walked down the gravel road toward Mavis and Dalton's house. Soldier Starke pumped Dalton with a thousand questions.

Where was he? How far was he from Virginia? Where could he get his hands on a musket? Were there Federal troop movements in the area?

Dalton tried to argue the point with the boy soldier, but he gave in and answered his questions.

When they approached the sharecropper shack, Alice Fae came running off the porch, sobbing, with tears running down her face.

"Oh, my baby, are you all right" She hugged and kissed Jessie.

The boy soldier became a statue.

"Dalton, who is this poor woman?"

"Play along soldier; she thinks she's your mamma." Dalton rolled his eyes.

"Since I have no memory of my real mamma that will be easy enough, sir," the boy soldier whispered.

"Mavis, get those bandages ready. Jessie's hurt!" Alice Fae yelled toward the shack.

Mavis appeared through the front door with a warm wet cloth. She placed the cloth onto Jessie's face. He grimaced but did not flinch.

"Alice Fae, will you hold that rag there while I talk to Mavis?"

Dalton motioned to Mavis while Alice Fae attended to Jessie. Dalton walked a few steps toward the porch and whispered.

"Mavis, Bully's done beat that child senseless. He isn't himself. He's been rambling on 'bout some guy named Pelham, I believe. Says he's a soldier and all manner of stuff.

Bully ought to be shot, and I just might do it."

"You better hurry or I'll beat you to it." Mavis gritted her teeth. "Alice Fae can't take much more; she's on the edge."

"Well, come on and let's get those two fixed up and put to bed. We better get Doc Grasson tomorrow."

———

"Whoa, mule!" Curtis wrapped the leather reigns around a bolt in the sled and walked up to Bully's house. There was a strange quietness. No Rover. No Jessie. No Bully.

Curtis leaned over the porch and looked through the open front door.

"Bully, it's me, Curtis. Time to git going, Bully!"

Nothing. Silence.

Curtis climbed the porch steps and poked his head into the door. Bully was where Dalton had left him, on the couch.

"Bully! Bully!" Curtis screamed into his ear. Bully stirred and rub his eyes. Curtis grabbed Bully and shook him with his stubby hands.

"Goddamn it, Curtis! I hear you! Give me a minute."

"Boy, Bully, you guys must've had a party here last night.

Looks like a bomb went off or something. Did you have pretty girls and everything?"

Bully rubbed his eyes and ran his fingers through his hair as he surveyed the chaos.

"Curtis, I don't know what we had here last night. Last thing I remember is being on the way home from the Talla-hatchie River. Where is Alice Fae and Jessie?"

"Bully, I didn't find nobody except you when I came up.

The dog ain't even here."

"Oh, my aching head. I think I'm dying."

"Well, you got to die at the barn, 'cause we got stuff to be doing." Curtis motioned for Bully to get moving. "Guess what I saw coming down here, Bully. That Willard fella you run around with, his truck is laying upside down in a cow pond like a big ole sow. Saw it this morning."

"Curtis, you sure?" Bully became more alert.

"Saw it with my own eyes."

Bully jumped up and went into the kitchen. He drew water from a galvanized water bucket with a gourd dipper and placed it in a wash basin. He washed his face and ran a comb through his hair.

"Let's go, Curtis! I want to see what you're talking about! I wish I knew where Alice Fae and Jessie could be. This place does look like a bomb went off, Curtis."

Curtis and Bully climbed into the mule sled and headed for the barn. When Bully and Curtis approached Rover's beloved plum bushes, they expected to see the yellow lab greet them with his customary barks of triumph, but, Rover failed to appear.

"Curtis, this is a strange morning, so far. Alice Fae and Jessie got out early, the house is a wreck, Rover's not showing up, and you're telling me Willard's truck is upside down in a cow pond."

"Right up here, Bully. Saw it with my own eyes. You'll see." Curtis moved into his tour guide mode.

Rounding the curve, Bully could see the tire marks where Willard hit his brakes. Hugh chunks of dirt were missing, and bushes flattened, where Willard left the road and went over the top of a barbed wire fence. Curtis brought the mules to a stop and Bully hobbled out to inspect the scene. He found a favorable place to cross the barbed wire fence that separated the road from the cattle pond. Sure enough, there Willard's truck lay upside down in about two feet of water.

"Willard, you out there! Willard, answer me!" Bully showed frustration.

"Curtis, carry me out there on your back. I got to take a closer look at that truck."

"Snakes might git us, Bully. I love animals, except snakes."

"Damn, Curtis, no snakes want you this early in the morning."

"You don't know that."

"Look," Bully picked up a stick, "I'll take this stick and make any ole snake pay if he messes with us."

"Promise?" Curtis asked.

"Yep, let's go."

Curtis squatted low enough for Bully to climb aboard.

Curtis staggered, trying to get his balance.

"Curtis, don't drop me before we even git started."

"You been eating too many of Miss Alice Fae's biscuits, Bully!"

Curtis grunted and groaned under Bully's weight. He regained his balance and trudged through the muddy water toward the helpless truck.

Bully whacked Curtis on the backside, "Git up, mule."

"Bully, if you don't knock it off, I'm gonna drop your crippled butt right in this here cow pond!"

"Ok, ok, Curtis, I quit."

Bully did not want to get wet. They made their way out to the ole Ford, and Curtis placed Bully upon the truck.

"Curtis, you see any sign of Willard?"

Bully looked down inside the truck as much as possible.

"Bully, Willard ain't nowhere to be found!"

Curtis reported looking through the truck. In an instant, Bully eyed the largest water moccasin he had ever seen. It made its way around the back of the truck straight for Curtis.

"Curtis, you love animals?"

"Except snakes, why?"

"Curtis, git up here on the truck with me, for a minute." Curtis turned to address Bully when he saw the moccasin.

"Mr. snake, don't git me! Mr. snake, don't git me!" Curtis came out of the water like a shot from a cannon. He landed on top of the truck with Bully.

Bully laughed. He reached out to offer Curtis a hand. Curtis didn't need a hand. He occupied the iron island of refuge, and held on to Bully with an iron grip.

"Damn, it, Curtis! I can't breathe. I can't breathe."

Bully fought Curtis off to remove his huge arms from around his neck.

"Bully, I told you there were snakes in this pond. You were supposed to scare 'um off."

Curtis sucked air and tried to talk at the same time.

"Well, Curtis, I was, but I didn't mean baby ones."

Bully caught a second wave laughter.

Curtis's hug for survival transformed into a hug of revenge. He locked down on Bully with all his might. Curtis become very, very strong with years of farm work.

"Curtis, please!" Bully went red in the face. Time seemed to stop for Bully. His eyes bulged. He mustered enough precious breath to blurt out, "Uncle!"

Curtis broke his death grip and began to lecture.

"Bully, you know I don't like snakes. You said you would scare snakes off! You said!"

"Yea, I know what I said." Bully inhaled several large quantities of air.

Meanwhile, Curtis looked for the snake.

"You think he's gone, Bully?"

"Yea, he's gone." Bully continued to recover from Curtis's bear hug.

Both Curtis and Bully fell silent. The sun started to warm, and the mules were getting restless.

"Curtis, you ready to git going?"

"What do ya mean, git going?"

"I mean, git to the barn. You said we had a lot to do. Besides, Willard probably walked home. Anyway, I want to check on Alice Fae when we go by Miss Lillian's."

"I ain't moving," Curtis replied, looking off into the distant.

"You ain't moving! How are we getting off this truck?"

"I'll die here before I git in that water with that snake."

"Curtis, that snake is a thousand miles away from here by now!" Bully said.

"You don't know that! Besides, he might have a brother," Curtis argued.

"A brother! Curtis, we got a thousand head of hogs that's waiting, we got five hundred head of cattle to check on, and five hundred head of horses and mules to feed."

"They are going to miss breakfast if it means me getting in that water with that snake."

In total exasperation, Bully climbed off the truck. He hit the muddy water of the cow pond and trudged through the water, cast and all, cursing the gods, snakes, hogs, and Curtis.

"Bully, you're going to get that cast wet!" Curtis hollered.

"Curtis, don't talk to me!"

Bully waded through the mud and water and reached the bank. The plaster of paris caste turned to mush around Bully's leg. He sat down and ripped the thing off in total frustration. He hobbled over to the mules and drove them out into the cow pond toward the truck.

"Curtis, get your ass in this sled and don't talk to me!"

"Bully, I love animals, except snakes."

"Curtis, shut up!"

———

Dust particles floated down long golden rays of light that found their way through the cracks in the oak boards of Carl's back shed. The faint outline of a body mixed with the shadows, shapes, and an odd collection of forms created by the random junk scattered across the floor

It was Willard.

Willard squinted his eyes, held his head and prayed to die.

The clanking of a chain interrupted Willard's prayer.

The door flew open, and the light exploded into the small darkened room. Willard fought the light with his hands. Voices came from the doorway.

Mizel and Junior, a two-hundred-fifty-pound gorilla of a redneck with a shotgun, entered the shed.

"Willard, you slept most of the day away. Mr. Carl wants to see you."

"What for? What about my truck?" Willard fired question after question. He struggled to get up from the hard-oak floor.

"Just get moving, Willard. Mr. Carl doesn't like to wait."

Willard's body recovered from the abuse of the hard floor with each movement. His head did not.

"Mizel, I'm starving. You fellas eaten breakfast?"

"Willard, it's ten minutes 'till two in the afternoon. You missed breakfast and lunch. There's no time to eat, now. We've got to go."

Junior poked the shotgun in Willard's ribs and nudged him toward the store.

"Junior, you need to be careful with that gun before you hurt somebody." Willard laughed.

When Willard, Mizel, and Junior approached the storefront, Willard noticed a closed sign over the door. Mizel knocked, and the door sprung open. Shotgun toting rednecks guarded the store's doors, shades covered each window, and the twenty-five to thirty member cadre of Carl's thugs milled with nervous idle chatter. When Willard and his attendants entered the room, dead silence struck. Willard tasted vomit in his mouth. Carl's famous "Jesus is coming" meetings struck fear in the bravest soul. He used these meetings to refine his bootlegging empire which ran on greed and fear. Willard once witnessed Carl beat a young man unconscious with an ax handle when he failed to repay a loan on time. Carl demanded fierce loyalty and strict discipline. Willard held on to what little denial he could muster.

Carl sat in his customary chair, which looked like a crude throne. He wore a small panama hat cocked over one eye; his shirt was unbuttoned, and a revolver hung under his arm. Mizel and four of Carl's cousins made up the inner circle. They owned the blood and shotguns and everyone else dropped their guns and knives in a former salt box near the door. The room overflowed with tobacco smoke, sweat, and tension.

Mizel and Junior brought Willard to the center of the circle to face Carl.

Carl rose from his throne and paced back and forth in a measured gait, looking at the floor in thought.

"Now boys, here we have an individual who has gotten on my shit list."

Carl addressed the crowd without acknowledging Willard or making eye contact. Carl whirled and back handed Willard across the face. Mizel and Junior caught Willard.

"But, Mr. Carl..." Willard tried to speak, but Carl drove his fist into Willard's stomach. Willard doubled over. Mizel and Junior held firm.

"Don't you talk while I'm talking, boy! That's

disrespectful."

Carl's voice rose and fell. He spoke through a twisted smile on his face. He loved the stage.

"Now, as I was saying before I got interrupted.... Where was I?"

Carl paced back and forth. He directed his attention to the 60-watt light bulb hanging from the ceiling. He rubbed his chin.

"Oh, yes, shit list. See, I carry this shit list and none of you boys ever want to get on my list. Well, this boy," pointing to Willard, "has gotten himself at the top of that list!"

Carl's booming voice dropped to a near whisper.

"A small thing, yet, a costly thing. See, I got to trust a man, or I get a little crazy."

His voice rose again. "I'm getting a little crazy."

The tension rose by the moment.

"See, this boy has done gone outside the circle and got all cozy with someone who said no to Carl Butcher. *No one* says no to Carl Butcher and lives."

Carl picked up a beer bottle and threw it toward the back wall of the store. It exploded with a shower of glass.

Ears rang with silence. A cockroach made its way across the floor. Everyone in the room knew Mr. Carl had referenced Bully.

"Now, I don't know which way this boy is leaning. Loyalty is everything. I speak it. Breathe it. Live it. Preach it. This boy didn't have his ears on. It's dangerous not to have your ears on around me. It can get you killed!"

A strange laugher erupted from Carl Butcher's gut. Willard's nose bled from the vicious blow across his face, and his knees struggled to support his weight. Junior's grip cut the circulation off in his arm and his head pounded. Willard looked around the room and no one would make eye contact.

He spent his whole life in the company of a few individuals in the room but now he felt alone. A short few moments ago, his concern was food; now it was survival. His denial abandoned him.

"Now, in my younger days," Carl continued to pace, "we wouldn't be having this little meeting. This boy would be floating face down in the Tallahatchie and that would have been that."

Carl paused for effect. "I guess I'm getting a little softer in my old age."

No one in the room believed that.

"I care about you boys like you are my children, and I want to see you prosper."

No one in the room believed that, either.

"I know everyone makes mistakes. I made one myself back in 1936." The tension broke and a roar of laughter went up in the room.

Willard did not laugh. Fear wired his jaws shut.

"Just to show you boys I've got a soft side, I'm gonna give this boy here a fighting chance to redeem himself. Mizel, git my chess set and that clock I ordered from the magazine."

Mizel jumped toward Carl's office.

"What's he doing?" a whisper came from the boys huddled together.

"Mr. Carl's going to *play* Willard," a young man spoke while an older one's hand grabbed the young man's mouth.

"See, the Royal game fascinates me because of the struggle. God knows I have attempted to instill a modicum of *culture* among you."

Carl's boys broke into laughter.

"Two opposing armies on 64 squares with the same intention: to kill the king. Kill or be killed is the brutal imperative that drives the drama."

Carl didn't know if his boys understood what he said, and he didn't care.

Mizel produced the board, pieces, and the double-faced chess clock. He set up the pieces. When Mizel finished, the two standing armies, one black and the other white, faced each other. Carl turned to Willard and looked him in the eyes. Carl's eyes were the eyes of a warrior.

"Son, I'm gonna give you a fighting chance for your life; you against me. You win, you walk. You lose, well, we'll just have to see, won't we?"

Willard jerked away from Carl. Junior's grip doubled.

"Mr. Carl," Willard spoke. "You...you... know there ain't no way I can beat you. Nobody's ever beat you in these parts."

"Boy, life ain't always fair, is it? I didn't say anything about fairness, I said you have a fighting chance. Now, if you don't want it, we can end this little meeting right here."

The boys in the room became more animated. Someone in the back shouted, "Play him, Willard! What have ya got to lose? Sides, you whipped up on me."

The boys laughed. Junior pushed Willard toward the chess table and the room broke out into a low murmur.

Carl picked up the chess clock and gave each clock ten minutes.

"Now, boy, this clock has got two buttons up here on top. One for me and one for you. When I push my button, your clock starts. The only way for you to stop your clock is to make your move and press your button. Then my precious time begins to slip away. Time is such a precious thing. Always remember that, boys. Time is such a precious thing. Son, if you look close, we got these little flags at the twelve spot on the clock. When the hands move within three minutes of doomsday, the flags are raised by the sweeping hand. Boy, if your flag falls before mine, and you have not killed my king, then I guess you lose."

Carl relished the stage.

"Now, we have twenty minutes, ten minutes each, to decide this matter. I guess this game can be called a *sudden death* match, so to speak."

Carl let out a laugh. He picked up two pawns, a white one and a black one. He placed his hands behind his back and brought them out.

"Pick a hand, boy. Choose an army."

Willard's hand trembled. He pointed to Carl's right hand.

Carl opened his palm and the black pawn rested in his out stretched hand.

"I get the first move, son. Gives me a slight edge. You better be scrapping, son."

Carl took a seat behind the white pieces and pulled his chair close to the table. Willard took a seat opposing the mighty Carl Butcher with a push from Junior.

"Mizel, would you start the game?"

Mizel walked over and pressed the button nearest Willard and the second hand on Carl's clock started to move. Carl thought for a few seconds and pushed his king pawn two squares forward. Carl's choice communicated a fighting mood. There would be no slow build up in the offering on this afternoon. A street fight approached. Carl slammed his hand down on his button, which started Willard's clock. Willard knew enough from the two years of playing every day since working for Carl that he had to challenge the center or die. He responded with his king pawn two squares and started Mr. Carl's clock. Carl pushed his king bishop pawn, a flank pawn, two squares, attacking Willard's foot soldier and offering his own. Willard knew Mr. Carl did not offer a pawn for nothing. Fear and greed battled for control within

Willard. Willard's hand reached for the gift. He withdrew it. Again, he reached for the unprotected foot soldier. With a shaking hand, Willard slid his pawn over and took Carl's sacrificial pawn off the table, while hitting his clock. Greed won.

"Well, son. You took my gift of a pawn. Just beware of gifts, boy." Carl grinned.

Willard squirmed. Carl brought out his king knight to a square that allowed it to attack the center and claim space. Carl hit his clock. Willard, wanting to protect his prized foot soldier, sent another one to support it and hit his clock. Carl brought out the other half of his equestrian force toward the front and attacked the center. He reached over and hit his clock. Carl's boys closed the circle around the board. Some broke away from the circle to whisper their thoughts and then return. Willard seized an opportunity to harass Carl's cavalry and pushed his pawn. Willard calmed down and got into the game. He hit the clock with authority. This harassment by Willard's foot soldier called for a response. Carl grimaced. He taught, lectured, and preached to his boys *do not waste time with frivolous moves.* Now, Carl felt obligated to punish Willard's chess sins. Carl thrust the attacked knight into Willard's territory for the first time, attacking the harassing pawn. Carl hit his clock. The crowd buzzed. Willard's eyes lit up. He grabbed his queen and sent her into battle attacking Mr. Carl's king. He slammed his clock.

"Check, Mr. Carl."

"You want to attack my king, I see."

The crowd stirred and came alive with excitement. They elbowed each other and whispered. Willard's toothless grin appeared behind his hand. Carl did not flinch. He took his fingers and pushed his pawn forward, blocking the attack. He reached over and pressed his clock. His eyes locked on to Willard. Willard, oblivious at this point, empowered by his ability to attack Mr. Carl's king, charged on. He captured the interposed pawn and hit his clock with authority. A subtle, yet detectable smile appeared on Carl's face-- a time of reckoning. He brought out his queen, capturing one of the harassing pawns, and attacked Willard's queen at once. Willard's legs bounced up and down; he bit into his lip.

"Looks like you want to promote that pawn of yours to a queen," Carl said.

Willard, two moves from this prized event, charged head-long. He would sacrifice his queen to gain another one. He advanced the ambitious pawn. Willard needed one move to queen his pawn. He pounded his clock. The crowd gasped.

"Check, Mr. Carl!"

Carl ignored Willard's comment and spent much of his precious time before he moved.

Willard looked around at the crowd. He and the crowd knew; Mr. Carl had lost. Carl's clock ticked away, but he paused to ponder. He captured Willard's queen and hit his clock. Willard captured Carl's rook and won the right to promote his pawn.

"I'll take that queen back, Mr. Carl, if you don't mind."

Willard pounded his clock and broke out in a big tooth-less grin for the first time. Carl's boys began to wink at Willard and communicate their glee.

"Mr. Carl, looks like you might have to get your pocket book out after this game!" A brave soul shouted from the back of the circle. Mizel cut his eyes in the direction of the heckler and showed his displeasure. Carl showed no reaction. He focused on the battlefield before him. After thinking for thirty seconds, Carl moved his queen one square forward. Willard's exposed king's defenses made porous by the adventurous pawns were threatened. Carl hit his clock. With one innocent move, the momentum and the initiative shifted toward the white pieces of Carl Butcher. Willard's desire to advance the pawn to its ultimate reward became his undoing. Willard's new queen floundered out of position. His king exposed to attack and his army out of position, Willard fought on.

The awareness of Willard's crumbled fortunes permeated the crowd and swept away his euphoria. Time ticked away with unmerciful precision. Willard, oblivious to the crowd, brought out his bishop and placed it on the square in front of his king. The boys buzzed with hushed conversation. Willard's bravado disappeared. His hand shook. He reached forward and pressed the button on his clock. Carl swept in with his cavalry and gobbled up the defenseless pawn. Carl hit his clock and once again stared his cold stare at Willard.

Willard thought, *my only hope is to survive his attack long enough to allow time to expire.*

He brought out his knight, attacking Carl's queen, and hit his clock.

Carl's flag hung. Willard's flag hung.

"I can't stand this," one of the boys muttered.

An electrifying energy pervaded the room. Carl moved with the precision of a surgeon. He lifted his knight and placed it on a square attacking Willard's king. When Carl moved his knight, a hidden attack by the queen materialized. He attacked Willard's besieged king on two fronts. Carl hammered his clock.

"Check!"

Carl's cold stare reappeared.

Willard's mind raced. The time pressure crushed.

Willard thought, *If I move left, it's over. My only choice is to move my king to the right.* Willard grabbed his king and shoved it to the right and slammed his clock. Sweat glistened across his forehead.

Carl lifted his queen and sent her into the back row of Willard's army, a sacrifice, but a brutal attack directed on the king.

Carl's boys let out a collective gasp. Carl banged his clock down and once again announced with an icy proclamation, "Check!"

Willard, with no choice, killed the attacking empress with his rook.

Willard hit his clock.

Carl's knight survived in the enemy camp. And for Carl, the powers of the knight were enough. He swung his knight over to a square attacking Willard's king while remaining unmolested himself. Carl used Willard's own pieces to trap the monarch.

Carl leaned forward with a twisted smile. "Check mate."

Carl's boys erupted into a roar. The bubble of tension exploded.

Carl nodded toward Mizel and Junior. Junior jerked Willard from his chair.

"No, Mr. Carl! I fought hard!"

"Yes, you did, son."

Willard kicked and screamed. He grabbed the center support pole of the store. Mizel and Junior tore him away.

"Aren't any of you son of a bitches gonna help me!"

Willard screamed to the muted room. Heads stared at the floor.

Junior struck Willard across the head with his pistol and Willard's body went limp. They drug him through the front door. The screen door slammed behind them.

Carl packed his precious chess set away with great care in its ornate box. He placed the clock in a protective cloth cover and announced, "Boys this meeting is over!"

SAY IT ISN'T SO...

Alice Fae awoke. The morning light filtered through the blue floral cotton window drapes made from used flour sacks. Mavis threw nothing away. She and Jessie shared an old cast iron bed her friend made available in a small adjacent room off the kitchen. Jessie spent a fitful night sleeping and Alice Fae stared at the ceiling when the first rooster crowed. Her mind raced with fears of home, of being a burden to Dalton and Mavis, of Miss Lillian's wrath, of Jessie's trauma, and of her anger toward Bully.

The smell of bacon interrupted her tortured thoughts. Mavis was awake. Alice Fae slid from the bed, careful not to wake Jessie, and covered herself with an old robe Mavis had provided. She made her way around the bed and stubbed her small toe on Jessie's Civil War books. She bit her lip, swallowed a scream, and opened the door leading to the kitchen.

"Good morning, girl." Mavis made breakfast. "Coffee?"

"That would be great, Mavis," she said, favoring her toe.

"Can I help?" Alice Fae offered.

"No. You just sit down and enjoy this cup of java while I rattle these pots and pans. Did you sleep?"

"A little," Alice Fae answered.

"Mavis, what am I going to do? I'm scared to go home. I don't have any other place to go."

"You hush your mouth, girl. You and that young'un of yours can stay here till the cows come home."

"I appreciate that, Mavis, but it ain't right. A body should be able to go home. I don't want to be a bother."

"Well, you can't go home till something is worked out with Bully. Somebody's gonna git hurt."

"I don't want Miss Lillian to find out. She might let Bully go and then we would be worse off. We are just making it, now. It's Willard's fault. Bully never acts like this, except when Willard's round."

"Alice Fae, you drive me crazy when you run off at the mouth like that. Hon, I love ya, but your thinking has gotten a little sideways 'bout that Willard character."

Mavis got louder despite her efforts to let the house sleep.

"Nobody's holding a gun on Bully when he drinks that Wild Cat whiskey. No one had a gun on him when he beat Jessie senseless, no one had a gun on him when he left those marks across your back."

Mavis threw a dish rag in the sink.

"But, Mavis, he didn't do these bad things when Mr. John lived. He didn't run with Willard then, either." Alice Fae attempted to defend her point. "There's got to be a reason."

"Hon, if you knew the reason, it wouldn't change a damn thing. Listen, if you're in a pen with a 2000-pound mad bull, why he's mad is of small comfort. How to get your ass out of the pen is a better question."

"I don't want out of the pen. I love Bully. He's not bad all the time, just when he's drinking that Wild Cat and running with Willard."

"Well, all I know is every bucket has got to sit on its own bottom, and Bully's getting worse and you can't fix him." Mavis said, "Alice Fae, Jessie's getting worse, too."

"I didn't want to bring it up last night, but you ain't the only one suffering in this deal. Dalton said Jessie wasn't making any sense last night. Like he was talking out of his head."

"Jessie's fine, Mavis. He's a good little boy, and he takes care of his mamma," Alice Fae shot back, surprising both she and Mavis.

Mavis shook her head in disbelief. She surrendered. Alice Fae clung to her point of view. Mavis loved her anyway. "Here, eat your breakfast. That hussy, Miss Lillian, will work you like a dog today. You're going to need your energy."

Alice Fae knew she frustrated Mavis. She wanted all this to go away. Jessie stuck his head into the kitchen.

"Mamma, where are we?"

"Jessie, darling!" Alice Fae got up and met Jessie.

He made his way across the kitchen. He clutched his Civil War books. She gave him a hug and brought him to the table.

"We're at Mavis and Dalton's, dear. How is your eye?" Alice Fae brushed the hair from the swollen eye and sat him in her lap.

"Ouch! Mamma, what happened to my eye?"

"You don't remember? Alice Fae looked surprised. No. A bear got you," Alice Fae said.

Mavis rolled her eyes and threw a pan in the sink. Dalton came into the kitchen. He rubbed sleep from his eyes with one hand and pulled up his bib overalls with the other.

"Hey, soldier, seen any Yanks this morning?"

"Mamma, what is he talking about?" Jessie asked.

Mavis cut her eyes toward Dalton. Dalton missed the cue.

"What am I talking about? You and me had those Blue Coats on the run last night." Mavis slapped Dalton in the back of the head.

He did not miss that cue.

Mavis fed everyone breakfast. Alice Fae helped Mavis clean the kitchen while Dalton finished dressing. Before Dalton left for work, he asked Alice Fae if he could have a word with her. Alice Fae sent Jessie outside to play with Rover, who had slept by the door.

"Alice Fae, it's none of my business, but I'm here to tell you, what I saw and heard from Jessie scared me last night."

"What are you talking about?"

"I'm talking about a little boy acting like somebody else. Alice Fae, he asked me what the dog's name was. He didn't know ole Rover's name. And today, he's acting like it didn't happen. Like he has no memory of last night."

"And Alice Fae, he doesn't remember Bully whooping him, either," Mavis added.

"What are you saying? That Jessie's gone crazy or something?"

"We're just saying that something ain't right."

"Like I said, Alice Fae, it's none of my business, but, if he were mine, I'd mention it to Doc Grasson," Dalton said,

"It's so embarrassing, though."

"Embarrassing or not, you need to talk to Doc Grasson, Alice Fae," Mavis said.

"Well, maybe." Alice Fae looked down at the table and played with her hair.

"And another thing, Bully needs to know he can't go off on you and Jessie without hell to pay. If it's all right with you, I'm going to talk to Jarvis and Cleo. They like Jessie, and Bully will listen to a two-hundred and fifty-pound field hand or two."

"Oh, Dalton, I don't know about that. I don't want any trouble."

"Alice Fae, you already have trouble. It ain't going to get any better by itself. Besides, you and Jessie got to get back in your house and it ain't safe left the way it is."

"I don't know." Alice Fae wrung her hands.

"Alice Fae, I'm going to talk to Jarvis and Cleo first thing this morning. You get to work, and Mavis can watch little Jessie. If you run into Doc Grasson, talk to him. He's a doctor."

Dalton stood up, gave Mavis a peck on the cheek and walked out the front door.

"Ain't he a stud, Alice Fae?" Mavis said.

Alice Fae blushed and took her last sip of coffee.

———

Willard regained consciousness to the stench of wet dog and exhaust fumes. His head banged on the floor of a metal dog pen with each pothole the old truck hit. Dim light filtered through a burlap bag over his head. Rope choked blood from his hands tied behind his back and the taste of electrical tape filled his mouth. When the engine throttled down, he recognized the distinct sound of a fabricated well pipe exhaust. It was Junior's truck—a 1949 Mercury cut in half and converted into a pickup truck. The truck crossed a wooden bridge, and Willard knew where he was. The cadence of the loose timbers impacted by the tires gave the clue; *the Lime pit.* He knew nothing good happened at the lime pit.

Willard thrashed and contorted his body in every direction in failed tries to free himself.

The truck came to an abrupt stop.

Willard heard Mizel ask, "You want to kill him, or do you want me to?"

"I can't do it, Mizel. You do it."

Willard heard the passenger door spring open. Footsteps approached. He detected the unmistakable sound of a 12-gauge pump action shotgun. Willard's muffled screams and struggle ended with double aught buckshot.

Bang! Bang! Bang!

Mizel threw an old tarp over the dog pen bolted to the truck bed and got back in the truck.

"You got a light?" Mizel asked. Junior's hand trembled and fumbled for a match in his shirt pocket. Mizel lit a cigarette.

"Let's go."

ALICE FAE'S REVENGE

Anyone of any importance gathered at Jill's Café, a popular hangout for the residents of Tupelo. Located across from the courthouse: bankers, lawyers, merchants, and country folk congregated each day for breakfast and lunch. The smell of country cooking mixed with the red and white checkered tablecloths and straight-backed cane bottomed chairs gave the hole in the wall café a place in the hearts of the locals. The heart and soul of the café belonged to one person: Beatrice Hogue. Beatrice's warmth and genuine charm attracted city and country folks alike. While she loved everyone, her first love belonged to her daughter, Jill, hence the name of the café. Many business deals culminated over Ms. Beatrice's ribs and a handshake. C.C. Bates frequented the café and intimidated most of the patrons, Ms. Beatrice excluded. Word spread about C.C.'s encounter with Miss Lillian's German shepherd, Killer. Ms. Beatrice played to the crowd with C.C. and the dog story. Some lesser brave souls joined in and C.C. Bates found himself the brunt of many jokes and exaggerations. The dog story would not go away.

C.C. didn't do himself any favors, either. He huffed, reacted, threw tantrums, and scoffed, which fueled the crowd's comments even more. One rainy Tuesday, Mr. P.H. McDonald and C.C. were having lunch when the country banker's old friend said the obvious.

"You know, C.C., this Lillian Watson thing has gotten way out of hand. It's got a hold on you like I've never seen."

"Don't mention that witch while I'm eating ribs, P.H."

C.C. looked around to see if anyone overheard their conversation.

"Well, all I know is you haven't been yourself since, and as a friend, I hate to see you lose your composure and make a damn fool of yourself."

"Nobody treats C.C. Bates like that and gets away with it, P.H."

C.C.'s pressured speech came through a mouthful of ribs.

"C.C., we went out there as good stewards of the bank. We had genuine concerns regarding our exposure. Lillian, well, you know Lillian. She's cantankerous anyway, and she's suffered a lot. It was an unfortunate incident. To her credit, C.C., she's almost got that crop out of the field, from what I gather, and she did it her way, not our way." Mr. P.H.'s voice of reason paled C.C.'s venom and the dense noise of the lunch crowd.

"You don't seem to get it, P.H. Nobody treats me like some low white trash, especially not a woman. This thing has gotten personal. If I let her get away with this, then every Tom, Dick, and Harry will do the same." C.C. remained impenetrable.

"Well, C.C., I don't know how good this is for the bank and business. I sure wish you could get this thing behind you."

P.H. fired his last bullet of reason. Then, Ms. Beatrice

walked to their table and addressed C.C. in a voice loud enough for all to hear.

"C.C., Tommy and Butch want to know if you'd be willing to loan a little money on a prize hunting dog they came across!"

Ms. Beatrice looked toward two toothless boys at a back table who grinned through a mouthful of ribs.

Mr. P.H. dropped his head in disbelief. His well-constructed argument for reason disappeared with one well-placed comment from Ms. Beatrice. C.C. came out of his chair.

"You boys just better hope you're not one day late on that damn pulp wood truck payment, and you best forget about harassing me about some damn dog. I'm sick of it!"

He threw his napkin and three dollars on the table.

"It ain't a German shepherd, Mr. C.C. It's a hound!" Butch yelled out from the back of the café.

The lunch crowd exploded in laughter. Mr. C.C. stormed out. Mr. P.H. shook his head.

———

Dalton had no luck meeting Jarvis and Cleo the next morning. But, while walking home after picking cotton all day, his ear caught the distinctive sound of an "M" Farmall approaching from the south. A dust cloud appeared on the graveled road, announcing the imminent arrival of machine and humanity. Dalton's mind snapped to Jarvis and Cleo. A covey of quail flushed from the nearby ditch bank. The red iron mule came around the curve with Jarvis at the wheel. Cleo rode in the exact position where Mr. John had died weeks earlier. Dalton waved down Jarvis A broad grin appeared on the field hand's face.

Jarvis spoke first, "Afternoon, Mr. Dalton! Y'all 'bout to wind it up?"

"I reckon, Jarvis. How 'bout you folks? I been watching your progress. Seems like you're making a good showing."

"Miss Lillian believes we can finish up by the end of the week. We be burning it at both ends, Mr. Dalton. Oh wee! Mr. Dalton, we all going to be glad when this crop is in the barn."

"Listen, Jarvis, I need to talk to you and Cleo for a minute. I won't take much of your time, but I need you to kill that motor for a minute."

"Well, Mr. Dalton, we can't be tarrying long, but I reckon we could spare a bit of time." Jarvis hit the kill switch and the Farmall's engine smothered from the lack of a spark.

Dalton moved to the rear of the tractor. Cleo and Jarvis joined him in the shade of the wagon.

"Jarvis, you and Cleo know little Jessie, right?"

"Yes, Mr. Dalton, he helps us pick cotton most afternoons." Cleo responded, with fondness in his voice.

"He's a good little worker and he makes the time go by faster when he's 'round. Come to think of it, I don't recall laying eyes on him today," Jarvis added.

"You ain't seen him 'cause Bully beat the hell out of him and Miss Alice Fae last night" Dalton answered.

"You don't mean it, Mr. Dalton. Lil Jessie is a mighty fine young man. He shouldn't be beat up on. He's just a young'un."

"That don't sound like Mr. Bully," Cleo added.

"Bully ain't been himself since Mr. John's passing," Dalton said, "He has beat Alice Fae and Jessie on several occasions, and there has been Wild Cat whiskey in him each time."

"Well, I don't have a thing against a nip of good whiskey from time to time, but a man shouldn't be going off on his family 'cause he's drinking," Jarvis responded.

"Well, what I want to ask you fellas is this. You know Bully better than me. I was wondering if you would be willing to have a little talk with him. I'll be there if you want me to. I got Miss Alice Fae down at my house. She's scared to go home, and I don't blame her. That little boy talked outta his head last night. It scared me."

Jarvis and Cleo backed up at Dalton's suggestion. "Mr. Dalton," Jarvis spoke as he took his hat off and began scratching his head with a grimace on his face. "It ain't normal for black folks to be messing with white folks' business. Especially when it be 'bout the chillens and women. Mr. Bully might just go off on us poor black folks, too."

"Listen, Jarvis, this ain't 'bout black or white; this is 'bout a drunk beating the hell outta his family."

"Why don't Miss Alice Fae git Miss Lillian to straighten Mr. Bully out?" Cleo suggested.

"Well, that was my first remedy to the problem, too. Alice Fae shied away from that one 'cause she fears Miss Lillian might let him go and they'd go from the frying pan to the fire."

"Why don't we git Rev. Strawrack to speak to him?" Jarvis offered up.

"I do believe that sun got to your head today, Jarvis." Dalton laughed. "That preacher ain't showed his face 'round poor white folks in Jug Fork since Bully put that shotgun to the back of his head. He just hovers over those lil' ole ladies round the quilting frame and hides out at the church. I heard he's even been turning down fried chicken on Sundays since that meeting. He is 'bout as worthless as a tit on a boar hog."

They all agreed.

"How 'bout the high Sheriff Bigelow?" Cleo offered.

"Hell, Cleo," Dalton spit across the road ditch, "he beats his ole lady from what I hear. He'd come out and give Bully one of his prize trophies. From what I can tell, we're back where we started," Dalton said.

"Mr. John would have Mr. Bully cutting firewood in July if he had his way 'bout this beating women'n and chillens'n and carrying on," Jarvis said.

"Well, Mr. John ain't here and the three of us are." Dalton brought the issue back to the point. "How's 'bout this? Y'all git this cotton up to the gin, git your supper, and I'll meet you in two hours at that lil' ole cattle pond where they found that Willard fella's truck. We'll give Bully a talking to."

"Cleo, I'm in. You coming?" Jarvis asked.

"My head's saying no, but my heart be saying yes. I'll be there."

"Cleo, you're a good man!" Dalton reached out and shook the big black man's hand. "Let's git moving."

Jarvis and Cleo climbed back on the Farmall. Dalton moved out toward home, anxious to see Mavis and share the news. When Dalton stepped on the front porch, Rover greeted him with a lick. Dalton could smell fried okra and fresh baked cornbread coming from the kitchen. When he entered the house, the smells intensified. Dalton felt starved. He found Mavis and Alice Fae sitting at the kitchen table.

"Hey, darling, what's cooking?

"Just the usual, sweetie. Some black-eyed peas, fried okra, cornbread, and some pork chops."

"Oh, that sounds good to me! Alice Fae, are you making it, dear?"

"I'm better than I was this morning."

"Where's Jessie?" asked Dalton, looking around.

"He's back there with his head stuck in those books of Doc Grasson's. I never seen anything like it," Mavis answered.

"Well, I was able to catch up with Jarvis and Cleo, a while ago, and we're going to talk to Bully, tonight."

"Oh, gee Dalton, I don't know." Alice Fae squirmed. "Maybe I just need to git on home and not do this."

"Alice Fae, there you go, again," Mavis jumped in. "Ain't nothing going to git better 'till something changes, and you're barking at the moon if you think things are going to git better 'cause you just show back up."

"Mavis, I'm just scared there's going to be some trouble or something." Alice Fae's chest blotched.

"Damn it, Alice Fae, there already is trouble. Besides, me, Jarvis, and Cleo just want to git Bully's attention."

"Well, I just don't want no trouble," Alice Fae muttered, Sweat formed on her upper lip.

"Alice Fae, there ain't going to be trouble unless Bully wants trouble." Dalton said.

Mavis called Jessie to supper and the four gathered around the table. Dalton lit into Mavis's cooking with a vengeance, while Mavis fussed over everyone. Jessie educated Dalton about the Battle of Fredericksburg. Alice Fae picked at her plate.

After supper, Dalton grabbed his hat, lantern, and shotgun. He kissed Mavis on the cheek and promised to return soon. Jessie asked where he was going, and Dalton said something vague about having to go see a man about a dog. He slipped out. The fall evening was crisp and cool. A quarter moon hung above the horizon. Bullfrogs and lightning bugs augmented the evening. A lone whip-o-will's call interrupted the sound of Dalton's boots moving through the gravel along the roadside.

Jarvis and Cleo were waiting when Dalton arrived at the cattle pond. The three men shook hands and moved out toward Bully's. If there was hesitancy about their mission, it was never mentioned. When Bully's house came into view, a single light could be seen through the front window. Smoke came from the chimney. Bully was home. The three men approached the house. Jarvis and Cleo stopped at the porch and Dalton climbed the steps and knocked on the door. They could hear Bully moving toward the door. *I hope Bully is not full of Wild Cat whiskey*, Dalton thought.

When Bully appeared at the door sober, Dalton breathed a sigh of relief. Bully seemed surprised at the sight of Dalton. While Alice Fae and Mavis were best of friends, Dalton and Bully, not so much. When Bully spoke, he turned to see Jarvis and Cleo standing near the porch.

"Hey, fellas. What you boys up to this evening?"

"Bully, this ain't no social call. We're here to discuss a situation that's got the three of us all balled up," Dalton said.

"Dalton, what the hell are you talking about?" Bully stepped out on the porch.

"Mr. Dalton be talking 'bout you going off on 'lil Jessie and Miss Alice Fae, Bully." Jarvis dropped the Mr. while addressing Bully for the first time in twenty-six years.

"Where is Jessie and Alice Fae?" Bully questioned.

"They are at my house, and they're going to stay there until we come to some sort of understanding, Bully. I'm sick and tired of seeing Alice Fae and Jessie getting the hell beat outta them and showing up on my doorstep. That's why we're showing up on your doorstep."

"I don't know what you're talking 'bout, but since when did niggers and poor white trash start messing in my family's business?" Bully said.

"Shut up and sit down, Bully." Dalton spoke. He raised his Fox double barrel straight toward Bully.

"Goddamn, Dalton! Point that thing somewhere else!" Bully complied. Jarvis and Cleo stepped forward.

"Mr. John would be seeing red with how you be carrying

on since God decided to take him to the other side, Bully," Jarvis said.

"God sure has a sense of humor," Bully laughed while looking toward the heavens. "He kills Mr. John, leaving me with that witch Miss Lillian. She takes me outta them fields and puts me in pig shit up to my knees. I can't walk like I used to, and I got more people putting guns in my face than Carter's got liver pills. I don't even feel like a man anymore. Sometimes, I wish it was me who had died that night."

"You shouldn't be bad mouthing God, Mr. Bully," Cleo said, speaking up for the first time.

"To hell with God, Cleo!"

"Look here, Bully," Jarvis spoke. "We all miss Mr. John, but we got to git on past it and move on. His passing left a hole that won't fill up overnight. We got to do the best we can."

"What if this is the best I can do, Jarvis? My knuckles have taken a beating since Mr. John died. I just go around hitting walls and trees. It takes the aching away from my gut for just a moment. The Wild Cat does the same thing."

"Problem is, Bully, that's not all you be hitting while you been drinking Wild Cat. You be hitting on 'lil Jessie and Miss Alice Fae, too."

"According to Alice Fae, you git crazy when you git that stuff in ya, Bully," Dalton added.

"I still don't know what you're talking 'bout. I ain't no saint, but I have no recollection of beating nobody."

"Well, I've seen the scars and you have too, Bully," Dalton countered. "I'm scared the scars you can't see are bigger, though, 'specially when it comes to 'lil Jessie. You need to get a grip, Bully."

"Look, Bully," Jarvis spoke, "Cleo and me been talked 'bout you not being in the fields and all. We believe that putting in a crop is harder than getting it out. If this farm's gonna have a chance of pulling through, we've got to get you in those fields next spring. You're the only one Mr. John taught to do the planting. Me and Cleo thought we might get our courage up and talk to Miss Lillian 'bout it. Fighting a wild hog is more inviting, but we all gonna be up a creek if we miss a crop."

"Jarvis, you know I'm dying down at that barn. I belong out there with you, and anything you and Cleo can say might just help."

"That don't change why we be here tonight, Bully. Cleo and me will talk to Miss Lillian, but you got to get yourself together. Fair enough?"

"Fair enough, Jarvis." Bully turned to Dalton. "Tell Alice Fae to git herself on home."

"So, Bully, we got a deal? You won't be going off on those two anymore?"

"Yea, Dalton, we got a deal."

Dalton stuck out his hand, and Bully shook it. Jarvis and Cleo extended their callous hands and Bully shook theirs, also.

————

Alice Fae was a nervous wreck knowing Dalton was down at her house talking to Bully. She paced back and forth, and blotches broke out over her chest and face. She rang her hands and muttered half audible prayers to herself. Jessie was back in the bedroom with his books. Mavis finished the kitchen chores.

"Alice Fae, do you and Bully ever have sex?" Mavis ask.

"Mavis! I'm worried sick and you want to talk 'bout sex! Shame!"

"Well, I never hear you talking about it or nothing. If a man whooped up on me, he would not be touching my damn waistband!"

"Well, Mamma said you had to give it to 'um or they would git mean as the dickens. I give it to him and give to him and he's still mean. I figured I wasn't doing it right or something."

"Alice Fae, do you ever do it 'cause you want to do it?"

"Oh, Lordy no, Mavis. Mamma would kill me if she knew I was liking it."

"Alice Fae, your mamma doesn't even speak to you, so what the hell are you talking about?"

"I swear Mavis, the minute I started to like it, she would know and come knocking on my door. I just know she would."

"Mamma, what are y'all talking about?" Jessie asked, poking his head from the bedroom door.

Alice Fae lit up like a Christmas tree.

"Ooh! nothing honey. You just enjoy your books, dear. Mavis and me are just talking 'bout girl stuff. Now, go on."

Jessie closed the door and buried himself back into his books.

"I would just die if Jessie knew we did it, Mavis," Alice Fae whispered. She attempted to regain her composure.

Mavis became serious. Her brow furrowed.

"It's none of my business, Alice Fae, but I wouldn't be bedding no man down until he was good to me. I enjoy sex with Dalton 'cause Dalton's good to me, and I like to be good to him back. Besides, I like how it makes me feel, and I don't give a damn what my mamma thinks. If he were mine, and I'm glad he's not, he'd be having to git his loving down at the barn until he was good to me."

"Mavis! Shame!"

Alice Fae headed for the door for some fresh air. Dalton walked in.

"Oh, Dalton, what happened?" Alice Fae blurted out.

"Well, Alice Fae, we had our little talk. It went pretty good, I thought."

Dalton reached over and gave Mavis a peck.

"Ain't he a stud, Alice Fae?" Mavis beamed.

"Dalton, don't keep me hanging, please."

"He got a little sassy, at first, but with about seven hundred pounds of white trash, niggers, and buck shot, he settled right down. He promised he would git a grip and quit going off on you and Jessie. We shook on it, and he told me to tell you and Jessie to git on home. That's about it," Dalton summarized.

"Well, I feel all out of sorts. On the one hand, I'm glad, and on the other, I'm scared to death. I won't know what to say to him," Alice Fae said to no one in particular. She stared out the window.

"Hell, Alice Fae, git on down there and work it out. He ain't no bear; he's still your husband," Dalton urged. "Besides, if he starts anything, you come see me, again."

"Dalton, you are a stud." Alice Fae pressed her blushing cheek to Dalton's.

Alice Fae again thanked Mavis and Dalton and retired to the bedroom to get Jessie and his books and to start the two-mile walk home.

"Jessie, darling, get your books and stuff; we're going home."

Jessie did not respond.

"Jessie, did you hear me? Git you books and stuff; we're going home."

Jessie did not acknowledge his mother. He rocked back and forth. A slow cadence sound emanated from his lips.

"Load! Ram! Fire! Swab!" Jessie screamed out at the top of his lungs. Wild eyed with gritted teeth, Jessie jumped from the small bed and repeated his mantra, "Load! Ram! Fire! Swab!"

"Jessie, Jessie, honey! What's the matter, honey?"

"Load! Ram! Fire! Swab! Git outta the line of fire, woman! "Load! Ram! Fire! Swab!" Jessie yelled.

Alice Fae ran into the kitchen where Dalton and Mavis sat at the table. They, too, heard Jessie's yells.

"Mavis and Dalton, come quick. 'Lil Jessie is talking outta his head or something. He doesn't look or sound like 'lil Jessie anymore."

Mavis and Dalton burst into the room where Jessie pulled the bed around to face the window.

"Load! Ram! Fire! Swab! Git outta the line of fire for the last time!" Jessie screamed. His voice was strong and compelling: his back ramrod straight. His chin was set, and his eyes were piercing.

"Jessie, darling! It's me, your mamma!" Alice Fae cried. She grabbed Jessie and shook him.

"Git this woman outta my line of fire or I will have her arrested on the spot!" Jessie shouted to Dalton. He ignored Alice Fae.

Dalton stepped in and pulled Alice Fae away from Jessie.

"Mavis, take Alice Fae out to the kitchen and let me see if I can talk to him," Dalton said.

"Alice Fae, come on, let Dalton talk to him." Mavis ushered Alice Fae to the door. She attempted to calm Alice Fae's hysteria.

"My baby! My baby!" Alice Fae shrieked.

Mavis managed to remove Alice Fae from the small bedroom. Dalton closed the door behind them.

"Sir, my name to you, is Private John Starke, serving under

Major John Pelham, Chief Artillery Officer for General Jeb Stewart, Confederate States of America."

"Not a problem, soldier, not a problem."

Dalton threw his hands up in deference to the boy soldier.

"We are in eminent danger! I need old rags for packing. I need more water for my swab bucket! Git those women to tear up this old bedspread. You, get me more water for my swab bucket."

The boy soldier jerked the bedspread off the old iron bed, exposing its feather mattress. He leaped across the room and grabbed the porcelain slop jar from the corner.

"Water, I need, water!" Jessie said.

Dalton stuffed the old bedspread under his arm and took the porcelain slop jar thrust at him by the boy soldier.

"Hurry! Hurry! I'll hold off these damn Yanks 'till you git back!"

Dalton left the bedroom with the bedspread and slop jar. When he entered the kitchen, he barked orders. "Mavis, you and Alice Fae tear this bedspread up while I go fetch some water from the pump."

"What the hell are you talking about, Dalton? I ain't tearing up that good bedspread. You gone crazy, too?!"

"Mavis, don't give me no mouth, just do as I say!" Dalton slammed the screen door headed for the pump.

Mavis and Alice Fae could hear Dalton pumping the long handle to the old pump out by the side of the house.

"I'm lost, Alice Fae. Let's just all be crazy and tear up this bedspread." Mavis's strong hands produced a rip and the two women went in opposite directions, tearing the bedspread in half. Alice Fae jumped with Mavis's every command.

Dalton entered the kitchen with a full bucket of water and chastised the women for their meager progress. He entered the bedroom. The boy soldier reloaded.

"Load! Ram! Fire! Swab!"

"Private John, here is your water and those rags are coming!" Dalton achieved full compliance with the boy soldier.

"You are a good man, sir! With folks like you, how can the Glorious South lose!" The boy soldier smiled. "Those Yanks have turned tail, so we can git our provisions ready, in case they git their courage up again."

"Listen, Pvt. John, let me git those rags from the women folk and then you and me can have a man-to-man talk. That okay with you?"

Dalton opened the door and Mavis and Alice Fae fell into the bedroom from pressing against the door.

"Dalton, what's going on?!" Alice Fae shouted.

"Well, soon as I can git those rags, we are going to sit down and have a man to man."

"Damn, Dalton, will you git off the rags!" Mavis barked.

"Mavis, darling, trust me. Remember, I'm a stud." Dalton grinned.

He collected the reconstituted bedspread, transformed into artillery packing.

"Well, don't be firing no blank, darling," Mavis retorted.

Dalton re-entered the bedroom.

"Pvt. John, these rags to your liking?"

"Perfect!" The boy soldier took them from his assistant.

"Pvt John, there's a guy you need to meet. He knows more about those damn Yankees and their whereabouts than any one in these parts. He's an old doctor by the name of Doc Grasson. If you are interested, I bet I could git him talking 'bout troop movements and stuff."

"He ain't a spy, is he?" The boy soldier raised he eyebrows.

"Oh, no! Pvt. John, he's got gray in his veins," *along with some morphine*, Dalton thought to himself.

"Well, when can you get me to him?" the boy soldier questioned.

"Why don't we wait 'till daylight and move out?"

"Isn't that dangerous, with Yanks crawling?"

"I got a secret path, so we'll be okay," Dalton reassured.

"If you don't mind, I'll sleep here with my gun and you wake me at first light," the boy soldier suggested.

"That's fine. You make yourself comfortable, and I'll see you in the morning."

Dalton rose and slipped out the door into the kitchen. Alice Fae jumped for Dalton again with question after question.

"Let him answer one, Alice Fae, before you ask him another one."

"I talked him into going with me to see Doc Grasson tomorrow morning. He wants to sleep by his bed, uh, gun 'till morning. I suggest you go on home, 'cause Bully's waiting, and I'll git Jessie over to Doc Grasson's in the morning."

"Dalton, I can't leave my baby overnight. He ain't never been outta my sight overnight," Alice Fae pleaded.

"Alice Fae, I don't know who is in that room, but I know one thing, it ain't the 'lil Jessie that I know. Now, we'll guard over him like he's ours and git him to Doc Grasson's in the morning. You go on, now!"

"Well, maybe it's better if I go home to Bully by myself, anyway." Alice Fae softened. "Miss Lillian will kill me if I don't show up in the morning. What about school? What about his piano lesson tomorrow? What am I going to do?!"

Mavis spoke up, "Alice Fae, you go on to work and I'll look after Jessie or whoever is in there. As far as schooling and piano, I say first things first. Let Doc Grasson look at him and tell us what he thinks."

"Tomorrow, I'll come straight from Miss Lillian's, Mavis. I promise." Alice Fae said.

"Now, git on down there and you and Bully work it out," Mavis replied. She walked Alice Fae to the door. Alice Fae faded into the Mississippi autumn night. She headed toward the "mansion."

Alice Fae's head spun. She needed the night air and the physical demands of the distance to clear her head. She reflected on her life and how others influenced her. She hated the way she approached the world. Along with the overwhelming fear of disapproval and rejection, she harbored great resentment. Alice Fae possessed no language to describe her feelings. She had enough resentment to go around, but most of it was focused on Bully now. She could not get Mavis's comment about not having sex with someone who was mean to you out of her mind. She never said no to Bully. Her inability to take a stand precipitated her early marriage, motherhood at thirteen, banishment from her parents, and the list went on. Her attempt to please everyone reduced down to her attempt to survive in the world. *In all my relationships, I am either one up or one down, mostly one down,* she thought. Her friendship with Mavis came closest to an equal relationship. Maybe that's why she enjoyed spending time with Mavis. Alice Fae's solace was Jessie. She sought refuge in his acceptance, hugs, laughter, and spontaneity.

Alice Fae lived in her head. She edited each feeling and thought, evaluated each situation, and imagined each future event, and then and only then, did she act. Alice Fae forced life through this mental meat grinder and the results was a kind of sausage to please. Alice Fae was sick of sausage. The gods have a sense of humor about such matters, however. Once aroused from the painless sleep of denial, we can never return. This is the purgatory of existence where we ride the fence. We're not in and we're are not out. The terrible danger is getting stuck in this place. The fence is uncomfortable, has sharp edges, and is unforgiving, yet it is the passage to freedom. Somewhere on the walk home, Alice Fae decided to make a stand. For once in her twenty-five years, she decided to place No in her toolbox of life. The scary part of saying No is you don't know what will happen next. It's this not knowing that is terrifying. It also is exhilarating. Alice Fae would be opening the door to possible terror and exhilaration tonight.

When Alice Fae approached the house, she could see Bully pacing back and forth in the living room. Her knee jerk reactions to Bully emerged, but she remembered her promise and focused on the whip-o-will in the distance. She took a deep breath and ascended the steps to the porch and opened the screen door.

"Bully, I'm home."

"Alice Fae, you've done it now. You run off and tell the whole world our business and I get a bunch of niggers and that white trash Dalton showing up at my door with a shotgun!"

"You should not have whipped up on us, is all I can say, Bully."

"I ain't proud of that, but you didn't have to go tell the whole county!"

"I didn't know what else to do, Bully."

"Where's Jessie?"

"Something's bad wrong with Jessie, Bully."

"What are you talking 'bout, Alice Fae?"

"He's talking outta his head, like he's someone else."

"Alice Fae, don't be messing with me."

"I ain't messing with you, Bully. It's the truth."

"Why didn't you bring him home with you?"

"He was too out of it. Dalton is going to take him to see Doc Grasson's in the morning."

"Nobody's going to be seeing after my boy, but me and you, Alice Fae."

"Bully, I'm real mad at you."

Alice Fae could not believe what she was saying. Her bottom lip began to quiver, and her skin blotched.

"What are you talking 'bout, Alice Fae? Spit it out!" Bully stepped forward with his fist clenched.

"I ain't backing down anymore, Bully. If it was just me, I might not be saying nothing, but it's Jessie, too. I think Jessie is acting the way he is 'cause of what's been going on around here, Bully."

"Oh, I guess it's all my doing, huh!"

"I can just take it, but I don't think Jessie can."

"You've always protected that boy, Alice Fae. He's going to grow up and be ruined 'cause of your coddling him."

"You're too rough on him and me, Bully. I don't know what has come over you, but you have become mean. 'Specially, when your drinking that Wild Cat. I wish you wouldn't drink that stuff."

"You drive me to it, Alice Fae. Living with you is like having two kids. You're scared all the time, fretting over Jessie and ignoring me, busting your ass for Miss Lillian and I git the crumbs off the table. When you want to talk to someone, you run down to Mavis, leaving me guessing what the hell is going on. Sometimes I feel alone as hell. Before I had Mr. John, now the only friend I can count on is Willard."

"I feed you and give you sex."

"Oh, great, Alice Fae—butter beans and dead fish."

"What are you saying, Bully?"

"All I'm saying is, Alice Fae, everything you do is 'cause you ought to not 'cause you want to. I know you ain't wanting me when we're between them sheets. You know how that makes me feel?"

"Bully, I was thinking 'bout what you're talking 'bout on the way home tonight. I ain't going to have sex anymore unless I feel like it." Alice Fae could not believe her mouth.

"You feel like it, now?" Bully smiled and reached for Alice Fae's breast.

"NO!" Alice Fae blurted out. Her heart raced; fear and exhilaration mixed.

"Now, ain't you are getting sassy! That just stirs a fire deep in my loins!" Bully advanced toward Alice Fae.

Alice Fae dug in.

"You just think you can have your way with me 'cause I'm your woman or something? You're going to treat me better or you ain't getting none of me, Bully!" Alice Fae glared.

"We'll just see 'bout them apples, 'lil woman!" Bully advanced toward Alice Fae, ripping his shirt off in the process.

"Bully, you stay put, 'cause I came down here to talk 'bout you and me!" Alice Fae retreated toward the fireplace.

Bully grabbed Alice Fae's blouse and tore it open exposing one of her small breasts and frail frame. He lunged again, grabbing for her skirt, but Alice Fae managed to sidestep Bully. He plowed into the stone fireplace.

"Augh! Goddamn it, woman! Now you're going to git it."

Bully staggered to his feet. He was met with the now sassy Alice Fae who armed herself with an iron poker confiscated from the hearth.

"I told you, Bully! You ain't getting none of me 'till you treat me good!" Alice Fae came across with the poker catching Bully in his aching loins. Aching took on a whole new meaning. Bully fell to the floor. A flood gate of rage sprang from Alice Fae. She gained the advantage. She struck

Bully time after time, and with each dull thud from the poker iron, she felt more empowered and savage; one for: her mother; one for Miss Lillian; one for Jessie's abuse; one for life in general; another for Mamma.

Alice Fae didn't know why she stopped. It quit being fun after Bully didn't move anymore, well, not as much. Alice Fae placed the poker in its stand and gathered herself together. She stepped over Bully's crumpled body and straighten the house a bit. *Look at that kitchen table, what a mess! Bully is such a pig,* she thought. *Well, Mavis said to get down here and work it out.* Alice Fae wondered if Mavis had her methods in mind. She felt exhausted and spent. Alice Fae retired to her bedroom and locked the door behind her. Tonight, she would sleep in her bed or die. The whole world could sleep somewhere else; she was sleeping in her bed.

WILLARD'S RING

Carl chuckled when he read the note. Why would the high and mighty banker, C.C. Bates want to talk to a bootlegger? Well, they do have a lot in common, Carl reasoned. A bootlegger and a banker live off others by skimming and taking a little off the top. They meet a need, provide a desired service, and satisfy a craving.

Carl pushed back his hat. He picked his teeth with an ivory toothpick. He would meet the banker, but on his terms. He scribbled a note: TOMORROW NIGHT. MUD CREEK BRIDGE. MIDNIGHT. He called Mizel into his office and instructed him to deliver the note to Bates.

———

"Where's mamma, Dalton?" Jessie ask.

"Well, look who's awake." Mavis spoke with a puzzled look. "She went down to you house last night. She's going to pick you up this afternoon."

"I thought you and me might go see you buddy Doc Grasson this morning. You game?" Dalton spoke up.

"What about school?" Jessie questioned.

"I reckon a little hooky never hurt nobody."

Jessie's eyes lit up. No school and he'd be seeing Doc Grasson.

"Git dressed and git your books together, and I'll feed you some breakfast," Mavis said. She cut her eyes toward Dalton.

Jessie ran for the bedroom.

"Dalton, it ain't going to help if Jessie ain't acting crazy. Doc Grasson's seen Jessie a thousand times. Hell, he birthed him," Mavis whispered.

"Well, all I know to do is git him over there. Maybe I can tell Doc Grasson what happened last night. It's over my head."

Mavis fed Jessie breakfast and watched out the kitchen window. Dalton, Jessie, and Rover walked across the bottom toward Doc Grasson's place.

"Jessie, who is Major John Pelham?" Dalton ask. He pulled a young stem of Johnson grass from the ditch bank and placed it between his teeth.

"A southern artillery officer."

"Is that it, I mean, is that all you know?"

"I've come across him several times in Doc Grasson's books. He fought under Gen. Jeb Stewart with distinction."

"With distinction! That's a twenty-five-dollar word for an old man like me, much less a puddle jumper like you." Dalton reached over and raked his knuckles across Jessie's head. Jessie laughed and ran ahead. Rover gave chase.

Dalton noticed Miss Lillian had all but finished the cotton harvest in the expansive field before him. Dalton knew he needed to be picking his own cotton today rather than throwing dirt clods with a ten-year-old and his dog. But Dalton thought, *I'm sick of picking cotton. I can use the break.* Besides, he was fascinated by the events that transpired last night. *Load! Ram! Fire! Swab!* Those words banged around in his head all night. *Damn, that kid can lay down a field of fire.* Dalton laughed to himself. *That kid almost had that bed as hot as me and Mavis can make one.*

As the land rose before them, Dalton's mind drifted to the people who must have walked this same path: the Choctaw; the Spaniards; the Yankees; the Rebs; the slaves; the share-croppers. He figured others would follow. Jessie and Rover waited for Dalton when he reached the road. An old peddler truck pulled over, and the driver talked to Jessie. Dalton reached into his bib overalls and pulled two nickels from his pocket. He bought two RC sodas. He gave Jessie one and he downed the other one. The rolling story pulled away and Dalton saw Doc Grasson's house through the dust. As they approach, Dalton noticed the Chevy parked in the yard. *Great! Doc was home.*

Doc stood in his beloved rose garden when Dalton and Jessie approached. Doc Grasson acquired quite a reputation with the local garden clubs for his prized roses. He minimized the accolades, yet even an inexperienced observer could see his appreciation for the recognition.

"Howdy, Doc," Dalton said.

"Now if that ain't a sight. A forty-year-old kid and a ten year old kid. You're short a dog. The two of you will wear one dog out." Doc loved to rib Dalton. "What brings you fellows across the bottom this early in the morning?"

"Well, Jessie wanted to trouble you for another book or two, and I wanted to speak to you, man to man, if you could spare the time."

"Sure, Jessie, you know where the library is. The door is open. Leave Rover on the porch and you help yourself to any book on the shelf. Come with me, Dalton. You can help me move a wagon while we're talking."

Jessie sprang onto the porch and disappeared through the front door while Rover took up residence in the shade of the swing.

Doc and Dalton walked toward the barn and Dalton related his concerns.

"Doc, I know you are close to lil' Jessie, and I wanted to let you in on some strange things that are going on across that bottom, yonder. Do you think it's possible for a body to be two folks at the same time?"

"Dalton, you ain't making any sense."

"I mean, could a person be one person and forget that he's another, and vice versa."

"If you are asking me if a person can have two personalities, the answer is yes. I've never seen it myself, but I've read about it happening. What's all this got to do with Jessie?"

Doc grabbed the wagon tongue and Dalton provided the muscle. With a giant heave, the wagon wheels moved. Once the inertia broke, Dalton spoke.

"Doc, I don't know much about nothing, but I believe lil' Jessie's got somebody else in him who comes out every now and then."

"Dalton, that's a pretty strong thing to say. I've been with Jessie more than once and never seen anything like that."

"Last night, Jessie lost it and acted like he was fighting Yanks and stuff. No, that ain't quite right He wasn't acting like he was fighting Yanks. He *was* fighting Yanks! Said his name was Pvt. John Stark and he was under command of a fella named Pelham, Major John Pelham?

"Have you heard of him?

Doc directed the wagon to a side shed attached to the barn and centered the doorway with the wagon. Doc dropped the tongue and the wagon came to an abrupt halt. Dalton leaned against the wagon and caught his breath.

"Yea, an Alabama boy, Jacksonville, Alabama, who was attending West Point when the Civil War broke out. He returned to Alabama and joined the recruits of Benton County. Artillery was his forte. He rode with Jeb Stewart and became the commander of the horse artillery. He became the darling of the South. Folks said he embodied every good thing the South was about. What has all this got to do with Jessie?"

"Last night, I was talking with a kid who rode with John Pelham."

"You don't say."

"Sure, as day."

"What's going on between Bully and Alice Fae?"

"They ain't getting along. Alice Fae comes down to our place every other day saying Bully's done whipped up on them. Me, Cleo, and Jarvis had a little meeting down at Bully's place last night. We tried to put the fear of God in him. I don't know how much good we done. He ain't been the same since Mr. John died."

"Does Alice Fae and Bully know you brought Jessie over?"

"Yes Sir."

"Dalton, why don't you leave Jessie with me today and I'll see to it that he gets home this afternoon."

"That's fine with me. I just wanted you to know what was going on. I felt as dumb as dirt in a box over this situation."

"Sounds like you handled it as good as anybody could, Dalton. I would be glad to run you back over to your place."

"No, Doc, that's fine. I'll just mosey back across there and get to the field."

Doc Grasson walked Dalton to the mailbox and again

thanked him for his concern for Jessie. After Dalton left, Doc retrieved yesterday's mail and walked back toward the house. Rover greeted the old country doctor with a lick. Doc entered the front door.

"Jessie, are you finding anything interesting?"

"Yes, sir, Doc Grasson, I can't believe the books you got!"

"Well, Jessie, when you're old as me, you'll have a lot of books, too, I'll bet."

"I just can't git enough, Doc. I could read all day."

"Listen, I had an idea. Remember me talking about poking around in that creek bed over at Brice's Cross Roads? Why don't me and you pack a lunch and head over that way and see what we can discover."

"Doc Grasson, that sounds great. What about Dalton?

"I told him to get on home and git that cotton outta the field. I'll take you home this afternoon."

"Great! Maybe we'll find a cannon or a wagon, or who knows." Jessie bounced up and down with excitement.

"You can't tell, that's for sure. Come into the kitchen and help me put something together for lunch."

Doc Grasson and Jessie placed peanut butter and jelly sandwiches, fried peach pies, and some molasses bread into a gallon pail lined with a piece of white linen. Doc rattled around in the pantry and found an empty half gallon Mason jar and made a batch of sassafras tea. He threw a couple of gardening tools into the Chevy, and Jessie guarded the bucket from Rover's curiosity.

Doc Grasson started the Chevy's engine and Rover leaped into the truck bed. They pulled out of the driveway and drove north to Highway 348. When he turned right toward Guntown, Doc Grasson's voice vibrated with excitement.

"Jessie, Highway 348 was called the Ellistown Fulton Road

during the war. I get goose bumps thinking about Sturgis's troops moving down this very road we are traveling!"

"Doc Grasson, you are the best thing that ever happened to me. I don't know what I would be doing now if I didn't know 'bout the Civil War."

"Well, you're smart, Jessie. I didn't have anything to do with that. Besides, I feel lucky to have met you and have you as a buddy. Now, when we get to Brice's Cross Roads, we got to use our heads as well as our backs if we are going to have any luck."

"I feel pretty lucky right now, Doc."

"Do you know what gravity is, Jessie?"

"Gravity?"

"Yea, gravity."

"Ain't it the stuff that makes apples fall outta trees?"

"Best definition I've ever heard."

Jessie grinned.

"Now, gravity doesn't take a day off. Not even to sleep. It's dependable, too. Another thing about gravity: it doesn't care whether you understand it or not. You don't even have to know its name. I guess the one thing you could say most about gravity is that it's steady."

"I fell outta the bed one time. Was that gravity's doing?"

"Sure was. The whole house was asleep. But, not gravity. There's one fella that's taught me a lot about gravity. His name is Einstein."

"That's a funny name."

"He looks funny, too." Jessie laughed. The Chevy pulled under a tree at Brice's Cross Roads battlefield.

"Now, where was I? Oh, yes, gravity. See, for the last ninety-three years, gravity hasn't taken a day off from this battlefield. Day and night, its total occupation has been to get the stuff that's on top of this hill down into that creek. Now, it got some of it down there on the first day of battle. Some of it, took fifty years or so. Some of it ain't down there, yet. I know which horse I'd bet on. Gravity will have everything in that creek. Then it will spend the next ten thousand years keeping it there."

"Doc, I git the picture." Jessie rolled his eyes and grinned.

"Now, I can talk more about gravity if you think I need to."

"Doc, please!"

"Rover, let me tell you about gravity."

Rover bolted across the pasture after a rabbit.

"The dog won't even listen to me." Doc laughed.

Doc and Jessie each retrieved a spade and shovel from the truck. Doc handed the lunch pail to Jessie and he grabbed the tea. They moved down the hill. The entire battlefield lay before them. They moved toward the creek with its hidden secrets. Jessie could feel gravity pulling him toward the creek, but he didn't say anything for fear of getting Doc started on gravity, again. Doc felt the tug, too.

Doc and Jessie set up a staging area under a huge bodock tree where they placed the lunch pail, tea, and their jackets. No jackets were needed after doing battle with gravity down the long grade. The creek appeared like a hundred other creeks in Mississippi: winding, serpentine affairs moving water from the hills, to the rivers, and to the sea. *Relentless gravity, again,* Doc thought. This creek had a canopy of cottonwood, willow, water oak, and hickory trees that created long shadows across the creek bed.

The sound of trickling water, an occasional croak from a frog, and periodic sounds of hickory nuts falling interrupted the serene silence. *What an incredible difference ninety-one years and a handful of months can make,* Doc thought. Doc's mind

wondered. He imagined how the water ran with blood, bravery, and fear not so long ago. A sad feeling came over him and
thought hit him: *not one living soul was alive today who survived
that battle. Gravity is not the only relentless thing in the universe,* he
mused.

"Jessie let's take our socks and shoes off and roll up our
pants. We might as well get down in that creek and get our
feet wet, so to speak."

"Sounds good to me. I love to git in the water, anyway."

"Now, we got to be careful, 'cause there may be a water
moccasin or two guarding the creek. Don't blame them. They
live here, we don't."

"I'll hit him with my shovel." Jessie crouched.

"No, we'll just slide around him and be on our way."

Doc Grasson and Jessie crossed a barbed wire fence with
their shovels and moved into the shadows and down into
the creek bed. The coolness of the creek bed could be felt.
Rover barked and splashed around in the water. Jessie
skipped a rock across a small pool. Doc surveyed the
terrain.

"Who is Pvt. John Starke, Jessie?"

"Never heard of him. Why?"

"No particular reason; rumor has it he was one of Pelham's
boys."

"Oh, yea?"

"Yea. Let's poke around over there."

Doc pointed to a flat bit of land between the creek run
and a small still pond. They began to move the silt, sand, and
gravel with their shovels and spades. Rover, on seeing Doc
and Jessie digging, began to help. He stuck his nose deep into
the mire, snorting and sniffing, then preceded to dig with his
front paws, throwing a shower of mud and sand between his
back legs.

"Slow down, Rover! You're going to hit China before lunch!" Jessie shouted.

Jessie and Doc laughed and continued to move the earth.

"Tell you what, Jessie. Let's git a little system going. I'll use the big shovel and make a pile. You take the spade and see what you can find."

"Sounds good to me."

Soon, Rover exhausted himself and lay prostrate in the hole he created. Doc found the wet earth easy digging and created a huge mound for Jessie's spade. Jessie attacked the mound of silt and mud with a vengeance. Doc encouraged him to search with care. Discipline would prevail, only to be over taken by excitement. Again, Doc's soothing voice would act as a calming agent to slow Jessie's actions. Jessie settled into a methodical and measured routine, which Doc Grasson praised. The two sleuths moved from site to site, employing their system with teamwork each time. After moving what seem like a ton of dirt, mud and silt, Jessie's spade hit an object that made a clank upon his spade.

"Doc Grasson, Doc Grasson, I think I've found something!"

Doc stuck his shovel into the wet dirt and moved over to Jessie's site. Doc pulled the spade from his back pocket and became Jessie's assistant. They searched the mound with great care. Again, Jessie's spade hit the object. Again, Jessie and Doc Grasson dialed in their hunt. Again, there was a clank. Jessie threw the spade down and began to work with his hands: dirt under the nails and mud between the toes. Out from the muck, Jessie pulled a small round like object.

"What is it Doc Grasson?! What is it?!"

Doc reached for his glasses and gave the object a thorough inspection.

"Jessie, my boy, you have found a .58 caliber Minnie ball.

My guess, from the musket of a Rebel."

"Wow! Are you serious?! Wait 'till I tell Mom and Dad! Let's keep looking!"

This scene was acted out several times during the morning of exploration and search. By noon, Doc Grasson and Jessie had found four Minnie balls, a button, a fastener from a harness, and an arrowhead.

"Let's break for lunch, Jessie. Gravity will hold everything here till we return. What do you say?"

"I'm starving, Doc Grasson!" "Rover, you hungry?"

Rover's tail said yes. The three moved down the creek bed to the spot where they entered the stream and scaled the steep grade. The lunch pail, tea, and jackets awaited their return. Doc Grasson spread the linen cloth on the ground.

"Dalton tells me your mom and dad haven't been getting along very well. Anything to what he's telling me, Jessie?"

"They're getting along fine, Doc Grasson. Reckon we'll find anything this afternoon?"

"Jessie, I know things are not great between your mom and dad. If you need to talk about it, I'll listen. Otherwise, I won't bring it up again. Okay?"

"Okay."

"Now, this afternoon, I thought we might move further up the creek near this bluff I know about. I've always had a hunch there would be some good digging around that bluff. Rover, you want a peanut butter and jelly sandwich?"

Half of Doc's right hand along with the sandwich disappeared into Rover's mouth.

"Sweet Jesus!" Doc jerked his hand from the starving dog. Rover wolfed down the sandwich and rolled his big brown eyes into the begging position, while waiting for another one.

"Doc Grasson, I think he's as hungry as me!"

Doc regained his composure.

"Well, he'll have to wait until we're finished. That dog is a bottomless pit!"

Doc reached for a fried pie. Rover offered him his paw. Doc unwrapped his sandwich. Rover rolled over. Doc poured some tea. Rover howled. Doc surrendered and broke his sandwich in half and rewarded Rover's performance.

"All right, Rover. Lay down and leave Doc Grasson alone," Jessie said.

Rover withdrew from Doc but maintained a watchful eye while the two finished their meal.

"Doc Grasson, Dalton asked me about John Pelham this morning. I knew a little, but not much. Who was he?"

"That's funny, because he asked me the same question. As I told Dalton, Pelham was a young artillery officer who embodied the best of what the South offered up during the Civil War. He was brave, fearless, and deadly with his battery. He gained the distinction of being referred to as 'the Gallant Pelham.' J.E.B. Stewart coined the phrase in one of his glowing reports, and I guess it stuck. He was very young at the time and was referred to also as 'the boy soldier.' He was about your dad's age during the war, maybe a little younger. He was the only soldier below the grade of general whom Robert E. Lee referred to in his memoirs. His ability first came to light at First Manassas, and later he distinguished himself at Groverton, Sharpsburg, and Second Manassas. For all his bravery and courage, he presented as a very shy and modest individual. He was forever ribbed by his peers and took it with good nature. Shy as he was, he was quite the ladies' man. He had tremendous leadership skills and motivated his men. Some of his artillery crew were boys themselves, but they fought with a tenacity that was unequaled during the war. Heck, ole Stonewall Jackson, who was about as stingy with praise as they come, even praised the 'gallant

Pelham.' Jackson was reported to have told J.E.B. Stewart that if he had a Pelham on each flank, he believed he could whip the world."

"Did he get killed?" Jessie questioned.

"Yeah, he was killed at a place called Kelly's Ford, in Virginia at the age of twenty-four."

"That's sad."

"Yeah, reports were that Gen. J.E.B. Stewart cried like a baby; said the loss of John Pelham was irreparable."

————

"Ya moving like an old man, Bully. Did Miss Alice Fae beat ya with an ugly stick last night?" Curtis questioned, while pouring corn into a trough and yelling over the den of squealing hogs.

"That's closer to the truth than you think, Curtis!" Bully shouted. He carrying two five gallon buckets of shelled corn to a group of ravenous hogs. His body ached, and his head hurt from being knocked cold and beaten by Alice Fae. While pouring the corn into the trough, the glint of a shiny object protruding from the mouth of a hog caught his eye. Bully didn't think much of the sight, but he became more interested when the hog passed up eating to hang onto the prize. After dumping his bucket of corn, Bully returned to find the two hundred pound red and white hog staring him in the eyes with the shiny object continuing to be visible. Bully moved closer. A devastating feeling came over Bully.

"WILLARD'S RING! THAT GODDAMN HOG HAS WILLARD'S RING! THE ONE HIS DADDY GAVE HIM!"

Bully threw the buckets down and jumped the fence and landed in the sea of hogs. The hunger of the hogs made them unrufflable. Bully made his way over to the hog, who tried to escape. The hog found the going slow due to the congestion of its comrades, and Bully overcame the distance. He ran his hand into the hog's mouth and gained partial custody of the ring. The hog and Bully held on for dear life when Curtis eyed the commotion and approached the fence.

"Bully, that hog don't look like your type!" Curtis shouted with his chisel tooth grin.

"Shut the hell up, Curtis, and help me get this ring outta this hog's mouth!"

"Bully, you don't know her well enough to give her a ring. You just met!"

"Curtis, you're a dead man if you don't stop running your mouth and help me! "

"Put your fingers over her nose and she'll let go!"

"Yea, and Ms. Lillian will invite us over for supper, tonight! " Bully replied.

"Trust me, Bully!"

Bully placed two fingers over the hog's nostrils and within twenty seconds, the hog relinquished the ring for lack of adequate oxygen.

"Damn, Curtis, I'm impressed."

Bully climbed out of the pen with the ring, limped over to a horse trough and washed it off. When the cold water washed away the grit and mud, Willard's beautiful turquoise and silver ring shined.

"Curtis, this doesn't make sense. Why would a hog have Willard's ring? He loves this ring and would never let it out of his sight. Something is not adding up. Where did these hogs come from?"

"That pen down by the road."

"Come on, there's enough corn to hold these critters for a while. Let's go down there and look around."

"The sheriff got Willard's truck outta the pond this morning. They still hadn't seen hide nor hair of him." Curtis said.

"Well, I don't like how this smell, and I'm not talking 'bout hogs, either."

Bully and Curtis made their way down to the pen, where they found three truant hogs, who missed their feeding.

"Curtis, that's strange. Why would those hogs turn down feed to stay in that pen?"

"Maybe they're courtin'."

"Maybe something else."

"What?"

"I don't know, let's just go see."

When Bully and Curtis climbed into the pen, the hogs came toward them. When Bully and Curtis's feet hit the ground, a very social white pig met them. It had a patch of blue plaid cloth in his mouth.

"That's part of Willard's shirt he wore the last time I saw him!"

"Bully, I'm not so sure I want to go over there."

"Curtis don't git froggy on me, now. Come on!"

The two men moved over to the spot where the hogs rooted around in the mud. A big black hog turned and a human hand protruding from his mouth.

"Jesus Christ! Oh, no. Not Willard, too!"

The hogs spooked and ran toward the barn with Willard's remains. Bully wrenched, gagged, and vomited in the mud. He clutched his stomach. Curtis provided what comfort he could, but he didn't feel too well, himself. Curtis moved Bully toward the fence and out of the pen. He returned to the spot where the hogs were occupied only to find a tremendous dark spot and remnants of much activity. Curtis knew that two hundred hogs with time could dismantle an anvil, not to mention a body.

"That goddamn Carl Butcher killed Willard! I know it!"

Bully spoke through snot, vomit, and tears.

"Then him and his asshole boys dumped Willard into this pen of hogs to git rid of the body. Carl knows a hog will eat anything!"

"We better git up to Miss Lillian's and have her call Sheriff Bigelow, Bully."

"To hell with Sheriff Bigelow! He's afraid of his shadow, not to mention Carl Butcher. I've got a shotgun and a slug with Carl Butcher's name on it!"

Bully turned toward the barn when Curtis tackled Bully and rode him to the ground.

"Curtis, what are you doing?!"

Bully came up fighting.

"Bully, Carl Butcher will kill you, Miss Alice Fae, and 'lil Jessie. He'll burn this place to the ground and pour salt on it if you try to mess with him!"

Curtis held Bully around his waist in a huge bear hug. Bully was no match for Curtis' strength. They lay on the ground until Bully exhausted himself under the pressure of Curtis's rock-hard arms.

"Curtis, let me up!"

"Not 'till you promise not to go after Mr. Carl!"

"Alright, Curtis, you win. But Carl Butcher needs a bullet between the eyes, and you know it!"

"Maybe he does, but that's not your job, Bully. Someday, Mr. Carl will get his."

"Now, let me up!"

Curtis's grip cut Bully's ability to breathe by the moment.

"You haven't promised, yet."

"I did!" Bully screamed.

"No, you didn't. You said *alright*!"

"Okay I PROMISE! NOW LET ME UP!"

Curtis released Bully and reminded him of his promise many times. Bully raked a large clump of mud off and hobbled toward the barn. Curtis followed.

"I still like hogs even if they ate Mr. Willard," Curtis muttered.

JOHNNY COMES HOME

After lunch Doc Grasson and Jessie took a stroll around the suggested site of the now famous bridge, which became the bottleneck for the Federal retreat. Doc Grasson encouraged Jessie to see the battlefield from the perspective of the Yankee teamsters who were overrun by hordes of screaming Rebel cavalry: the desperation of being cut off from an avenue of retreat; the dilemma of whether to abandon their wagon and try to save their hide; or whether to be heroic and try to save both their hide and their wagon. Many wagons were abandoned based on the outcome of that very decision. After the promenade around the battlefield, Doc Grasson and Jessie returned to their last site, gathered up their tools and moved further upstream toward the bluff. When the two explorers and Rover rounded a curve in the creek, their eyes gazed upon a twelve to fifteen-foot reddish bluff jutting out on the east side of the creek. Below the bluff, huge clusters of blackberry vines and sage grass covered most of the terrain down to the water's edge. Doc Grasson did not remember the quantity of vegetation being so great. The thicket was old and well established.

"I should have brought an axe to negotiate this obstacle, Jessie. We've got our work cut out for us if we're going to have a chance for Lady Luck to smile."

"Yea, look at all the stickers!"

"Let me get in there with the shovel and see if I can clear us a little working space."

Doc Grasson made his way into the middle of the thicket and used his shovel to cut the bottoms off the blackberry vines. After much effort, he secured a foothold on the thicket and cleared a ten to twelve-foot plot suitable for digging. After a short break, for Doc Grasson to catch his breath, he and Jessie relocated their tools onto the site and moved the reluctant earth. Roots, grubs, and an occasional field mouse's den all came under the intrusion and violation of Doc Grasson's shovel. Doc moved enough earth to fill his pickup truck when his shovel stopped. He took his spade from his pocket and explored with care. When he pulled away the earth, a metallic object appeared.

"Jessie, get over here on the double. Lady Luck is smiling."

"What is it, Doc Grasson?"

"I'm not sure, but my gut tells me it's a find."

When Doc Grasson brushed more of the earth away, there appeared a soldier's belt buckle; it was intact. Doc Grasson continued to clean away the dirt, and raised letters began to appear. The three letters were CSA. Doc Grasson and Jessie became very quiet. They both were very excited yet awed by the experience.

"I don't believe this, Doc Grasson. We have found a Confederate belt buckle."

"Jessie, you are so right. Lady Luck is smiling today.

Remember my saying that we would have to use our heads as well as our backs to entice Lady Luck's favors?"

"Yes, sir."

"This bluff has fascinated me for years. I always could imagine a soldier falling off this bluff and somehow getting passed over in the drama of chasing Yanks toward Memphis. Either we have found an isolated article, or we are on the threshold of finding more. Let's keep digging."

Doc and Jessie continued to work their system of Doc moving the dirt and Jessie using the spade to search for treasures. As the afternoon wore on, they found the remnants of what appeared to be a canteen. The discovery fueled the desire to continue digging. Doc Grasson and Jessie discussed school, war, girls, dogs, food, and music. Each time Doc broached family or home, Jessie refused to talk and would retreat within himself. Doc would move on to another subject and Jessie would make himself available and enter the conversation with glee.

When the shadows became long and their bodies tired, Doc Grasson and Jessie resigned themselves to the fact: they were not going to find more on this afternoon.

"Jessie, why don't we call it a day and get over to your place? We've had a pretty good run of luck, and we'll come back to dig another day."

Jessie's smile dropped and the little boy looked saddened by the country doctor's suggestion. Doc knew Jessie was reluctant to end the day. Jessie moved in the direction of Rover.

The golden Lab dug after a field mouse in a clump of vines and bushes adjacent to the area that had been cleared by Doc Grasson.

"Rover, come on, boy! Don't make me have to come get you! Doc Grasson, that dog has a mind of his own!"

"Yea, he's the only one who has any fight left in him."

Jessie went over to the thicket where Rover busied himself. He threw dirt and grass into the air with intermittent snorts into the earth with his long, wet nose. When Jessie entered the thicket, his eyes widned.

"Doc! Doc! Come quick!" Jessie's voice rang with new found excitement and energy.

"What have you two stirred up, now?" Doc questioned.

When Doc approached the focus of the commotion, he saw Jessie down on his hands and knees fighting Rover for position, and both were digging and throwing a cascade of dirt into the long shadows of the afternoon.

"You boys got your second wind, I see!"

"Doc, look!" Jessie moved his body revealing an exposed human skull. It starred into Doc's eyes.

"Lady Luck ain't through with us yet, is she!" Doc shouted.

He moved in closer.

"Okay, you two, slow down, slow down! This is a place for a scalpel, not a cross cut saw!"

Jessie grabbed Rover and the two rolled over into the grass, away from the fallen warrior. Rover put up a violent struggle but succumbed to his master's restraint and urgings. Doc Grasson approached the dead soldier with the reverence and care he would have provided a sick child.

"Ole fella, you have waited a long time for this day. For years, my gut told me you were down here, and I'm sorry I waited this long to listen."

Doc Grasson removed his spade from his back pocket and began the careful task of removing the rich sandy loam earth that encased the unfortunate fighter. Doc Grasson's trained eye gauged the soldier to be no more than nineteen or twenty by the condition of the skull and the teeth: a mother's son; a waiting girl's boyfriend or husband. Someone's ultimate gift to the universe, shot dead and left like a dog on the side of the road. The slow removal of earth revealed the intact remains of a young Confederate soldier sporting the CSA buckle. When Doc Grasson and Jessie removed the reluctant earth, they were in for another sunrise. The soldier's right hand hung faithfully to his .58 caliber Springfield for close to a century. Doc Grasson removed the rusted yet intact piece from the soldier's hand. Further digging revealed the remains of a canteen and the fallen soldier's watch.

"Doc Grasson, I can't believe this day," Jessie said.

"We have shared in the personal history of this fine young man, Jessie. We have a duty to see that he has a proper burial."

"How can we do that?"

"Well, I'm not sure just yet, Jessie. I'll have to think about it. Right now, we must be concerned with getting him out of this creek bed. You and Rover run up to the picnic tree and get our blanket. We'll use it to bring Johnny out."

Jessie and Rover disappeared around the bend. They sprinted after the blanket. Doc sat alongside Johnny Reb. The darkness swallowed the light.

"You know Johnny, we southern folks haven't been the same since that nasty little disagreement concerning the Cause. The wounds are still deep and painful. Close to a century of sand has cascaded through that cruel and relentless hourglass, and the wounded feelings are just under the surface of our being, waiting to pop like a coiled spring with the slightest provocation. Your fight, well, at least it was more to the point and nobler. Ours, I'm sorry to say, has been a vain search for dignity and direction in the mist of ruins. A lot has happened while you have been resting in this ditch, son. Most of the South's finest young men were slaughtered, like your-self. You boys took quite a few Yanks with ya, I might add. Then the southern occupation by every crook and two-bit profiteer money or influence could buy. A major Depression, two World Wars and several smaller wars, including fighting in some place called Korea, as I speak. I guess you can say we just haven't gotten back on our feet yet."

Doc Grasson paused while staring at the clear stream of water trickling through the sandy rocks.

"We don't git to pick when we're born, do we, Johnny?" Doc sighed and muttered to himself, "Just time and chance. Just time and chance."

While Doc sat with Johnny Reb in the creek bed at Brice's Cross Roads, he thought back on his own life and felt a pang of sadness. How he missed his darling wife Olga and many of his ole friends who had long died in this war, that accident, or worse yet, of old age.

Doc was brought back to the present by sounds of Rover barking and water splashing from around the bend. Doc wondered about Jessie and how his life might unfold—again, it was just time and chance. Jessie didn't get a vote either.

Doc Grasson and Jessie laid Johnny Reb on the blanket along with his belongings and headed toward the truck. Dark-ness replaced the light of day. Doc and Jessie were assisted by a full moon, which made their plight easier. Doc Grasson turned the Chevy toward Bully's place. He noticed Jessie retreated into that darkness where fear is a relentless stalker. Doc made several attempts at conversation, but the closer to home, Jessie retreated into the world of his solitude: the slow rocking back and forth; the occasional utterances; then more silence.

Doc turned the Chevy into the "mansion" drive and saw a

shadeless light hanging over the table and casting diffused amounts of light through the adjacent windows. Rover barked when the Chevy came to a stop near the front porch. Alice Fae appeared at the screenless front door, and a broad smile crossed her face with the recognition of the Chevy. Rover hit the ground, and with one bound, he was on the porch and greeting Alice Fae.

She returned the greeting with a brisk scratch behind Rover's ears.

Jessie became more animated when his keen sense of observation assessed the absence of Bully.

"Mamma, you won't believe what me and Doc Grasson found today. Come see! Come see!"

"Hello, Doc Grasson. From the looks of Jessie, you guys had a big day."

"You might say Lady Luck smiled on us today, and we brought one of our own home."

"Mamma, look!" Jessie pulled back the blank.

"Oh, my goodness! What on earth!" Alice Fae shrieked.

"Jessie and I played a long-standing hunch and found this brave young man lying in the creek bed over at Brice's Cross Roads. He's about ninety-four years late for supper. "

"Speaking of supper, Mamma, I'm starving. You hungry, Doc Grasson?"

"You and your mamma get in the house before this chill gets both of you. I need to lay Johnny Reb to rest and head on home. Alice Fae, I'll be talking to you." Doc gave her a reassuring wink and climbed into the Chevy.

"Be glad for you to stay for supper, Doc Grasson," Alice Fae offered, praying Doc would not take her offer.

"Thanks, again, Alice Fae, some other time."

Doc turned the Chevy around and saw Jessie and Alice

Fae waving through his rear-view mirror. Doc let out a long sigh and turned the toward Birmingham Ridge and home. Tonight, Doc Grasson's heart felt empty as the eyes of Johnny Reb.

BANKER MEETS BOOTLEGGER

"Git your citified ass out here on the double, Sheriff!" Miss Lillian raved. "I got dead men showing up in my hog pens and live one's standing around talking 'bout the dead ones. Hogs aren't getting fed and who in hell knows how many sick hogs I'll have over this foolishness!"

Curtis and Bully could hear Miss Lillian raging from the back porch; where they held the mules and played with Killer.

"First thing in the morning!" Miss Lillian screamed.

The mules jerked and Killer ran off the porch and hid behind a pecan tree. Curtis and Bully heard the phone crash down. Miss Lillian kicked an empty water bucket. It banged hard against the screen door.

"Boys!" Miss Lillian barked. Curtis and Bully jumped.

"Yes'um!" the two responded in complete unison.

Miss Lillian ran out of the back door with her coat and pistol.

"Meet me at the barn!" she ordered. "That total waste of humanity for a sheriff fears his shadow. Said something 'bout one of Carl Butcher's boys missing and wanted to go slow!"

"I told you, Curtis! Sheriff Bigelow won't do a damn thing 'bout Willard. He's scared!" Bully seethed.

Miss Lillian jumped into her Oldsmobile and drove off before Bully and Curtis could get the mules turned around. When they arrived at the barn, Miss Lillian stood at the site of Willard's reluctant re-entry into the food chain. Bully and Curtis pulled the mules up to the fence and jumped into the pen.

"Nutt'en but a greasy spot, Miss Lillian!" Curtis commented.

"Bully let me make sure I got this straight. You say this was that Willard fella? The one who rode the roads in that old black Ford pickup?"

"Yes'um!"

"He was nothing but low life white trash, but nobody deserves an ending like this. Not in one of my hog pens! You think Carl Butcher, that bootlegging crook, had something to do with this, don't you, Bully?"

Bully told Miss Lillian the story of his "business meeting" with Carl and his desire to own Mr. John's land. Miss Lillian's lips turned blue. The color drained from her face.

"We'll just see about that." Miss Lillian spoke very slow and with a deep hatred.

While the three stood staring at the bloody spot, a commotion arose from their flank. Miss Lillian wheeled to see a 500 lb. boar hog charging, tusk flashing, and mouth foaming. Without thought or hesitation, she shot the hog dead in its tracks. The hog's momentum carried it forward knocking Curtis off his feet and into the mud.

Miss Lillian placed her pistol back into her coat pocket and headed for the Oldsmobile.

"Bully help Curtis up and y'all dress that hog. The taste of blood makes a hog do crazy things."

As Bully helped Curtis to his feet, Miss Lillian climbed the fence, placed her boots in the trunk of the Oldsmobile and drove off.

"She just killed my favorite hog, Bully!" Curtis shook his head in bewilderment.

Screw hogs, Bully thought. He wanted to see Carl Butcher dead.

———

Carl Butcher leaned against the dew drenched rusty iron banister of Mud Creek Bridge. He filled his lungs with the cool night air of autumn. He pulled a can of Prince Albert tobacco from his shirt pocket and began a series of ritualistic moves most country folks called "rolling your own." His left index finger made a perfect trough in the rolling paper. His right hand shook the precise amount of tobacco from the thin red can. He closed the lid with the same hand and placed it back into his shirt pocket. He placed his right index finger into the opposite end of the paper trough filled with the rich aromatic tobacco, and with an expert twist born of thousands of repetitions, a perfect cigarette materialized in the darkness. He ran his wet tongue down the paper seam to secure the structural integrity of his masterpiece and placed it between his puffy red lips. With a confident flick of his rough thumbnail, a match exploded in the Mississippi night illuminating a face as hard as the steel banister he leaned against.

Carl hated C.C. Bates. Carl's mouth had problems forming the necessary muscular requirement to emit a C when thinking of Bates; to repeat the vile task twice was heroic. Carl remembered C.C. Bates in grade school. Bates was a snotty nosed kid who thought he was better than everyone else. He humiliated Carl in front of the class, ridiculing him over his clothes, which were worn yet clean. The class exploded in laughter and Carl ran all the way home in tears. Carl never forgot that moment and refreshed the wound by replaying the memory in vivid detail. Carl's eyes locked on the lights interrupting the darkness from the east.

The approaching lights blinked twice in rapid succession. Carl knew it was Mizel. Carl created a mile-wide perimeter around the Mud Creek Bridge with his boys armed with shotguns and automatic rifles. He instructed Mizel to intercept the banker. Carl knew how to avoid an ambush. Mizel's truck rolled to a stop. Carl released the cocked hammer on his Colt .38. Mizel drug the terrified banker from the truck and escorted him to the center of the bridge where Carl stood.

"Evening Bates!" Carl's acid voice would have dissolved a hub cap.

Bates attempted to utter a response, but his dry mouth and swollen tongue were paralyzed.

"Mizel, good job. You take the boys and head on back to the store. I believe Mr. Bates and I can handle the rest of this evening."

"Yes, sir." Mizel smiled.

Carl pulled his ivory toothpick from his shirt pocket and punished Bates with an eerie and uncomfortable silence. Carl picked around his gold tooth. The only competing sounds were the occasional ripple from the water below, Mizel going through the gears in the distance, or the faint sound of the dew dripping from the banisters and hitting the thick oak bridge decking.

"I have half a mind to put a bullet in your head, Bates." Carl spoke. His voice calm like requesting the salt from across the table. He looked off into the night.

Bates started to speak. Carl back handed the poor banker across the mouth.

"Don't interrupt me while I'm talking, you son of a bitch!"

Spit and snot flew from Bates. His head recoiled from Carl's powerful blow. A small rivulet of blood trickled past his quivering lip.

Carl collected his thoughts.

"You have entered my world, Bates. I make the rules in this world. I call the shots, and what I say happens! Do you understand that, Bates?"

Mr. C.C was afraid to speak, and he was afraid not to speak.

"You better answer me before I pinch your miserable little head off, Bates! "

"I-I hear you, Carl!"

Carl grabbed the unfortunate banker and lifted him off the oak flooring of the bridge, his head banging hard against the iron railing. Carl's nose touched Mr. C.C.'s nose. Carl's ivory toothpick penetrated the banker's cheek, creating another crimson rivulet across the terrified banker's face.

"That's Mr. Butcher! Mr. Carl Butcher, Bates!"

"Yes, Mr. Butcher! Yes, Carl, I-I mean Mr. Carl! No, Butcher, Mr. Butcher!"

Carl Butcher brought Mr. C.C. back down to where his scuffed shoes touched the bridge flooring once again. Carl straightened the banker's suit and tie in a condescending fashion. Mr. C.C. attempted to control the blood running from his face with a handkerchief.

"Now that you and I have a general understanding concerning the nature of our relationship, Bates, what do you want to talk about?"

"Mr. Butcher," C.C. stammered. He attempted to regain what little composure and dignity he had left. "I hear through the grapevine that you are interested in Lillian Watson's land."

"What if I was?"

"I'm willing to help you acquire the property," the banker replied with great caution.

"Who knows you're here, tonight, Bates?" Carl questioned.

"No one, Car, -uh... Mr. Butcher." Mr. C.C. froze.

The reoccurring thought of putting a bullet into the banker's head kept interrupting Carl's concentration.

"What makes you think I'd need your help if I wanted her property?" Carl shot back.

"Not too many people I know could buy 3000 acres without a little help, even if the property was for sale, which it's not."

Mr. C.C. felt more comfortable entering his world of deal making.

"What kind of help did you have in mind, Bates?"

"You help me undermine that widow woman's efforts to make a go of it, I'll foreclose on the land, and give you a low interest loan when it sells at the courthouse." C.C. disclosed his burning desire to destroy the woman responsible for his public humiliation.

"You're an idiot, Bates!" Carl replied. A cruel grin erupted across his face. "One, I wouldn't need one red dime of your city money to buy that place if I wanted it. Two, you're showing me what a pathetic small weasel you are, letting an old widow woman get your goat enough to risk life and limb in the middle of the night, talking to the meanest son of a bitch in this county."

"I want that bitch off that land and I don't care what it takes!"

C.C. reconnected with the fire in his belly.

"I have bigger fish to fry, Bates." Carl's business mind moved.

"What are you talking about?"

"I can get the widow woman off that place, but you're a little light on your end of the deal." Carl countered the banker's offer.

"Foreclosing on the property and offering you a low interest loan is not what I call a light offer." C.C. got his courage up a bit.

"One, I don't need your money. Two, the land would have to be foreclosed on if she failed to pay her land payments, and no one is going to bid against Carl Butcher. Three, I don't need you to create hell in that old woman's life. Me and my boys can cover that end of it, I reckon. No, if you want my help in this deal, you are still a little short."

"What are you angling at?" Mr. C.C. asked. His nervousness returned

"I want that piss ant of a sheriff off my ass, and I want Buford King's head delivered to me in a flour sack."

"Christ, Carl! I mean Mr. Butcher!" C.C. recanted, backing up. "Buford King is just as notorious as you are when it comes to running whiskey and putting the fear of God in folks. What makes you think I could influence him one way or another?" C.C. questioned. A new alarm sounded in his voice.

"I know for a fact he owes your bank a considerable amount of money. I win at poker, he doesn't." Carl smiled.

"You expect me to gun him down and bring you his head?! I'm a banker, not a killer!"

Carl laughed. "Get the high Sheriff Bigelow to do it for you. You got him in you back pocket."

"He's afraid of his shadow; you know that better than anyone." Bates said. He saw his deal and night's work coming unraveled.

"I tell you what, Bates. Me and my boys will do the dirty

deed for the county. Being as civic minded as we are, you set King up and my boys will rid the county of one less bootlegger."

Mr. C.C. ran his hand through his thinning hair and wiped the sweat off his forehead.

"I don't like it, but you've got a deal, Mr. Butcher. Buford King for running old lady Watson of that land." C.C. extended his hand.

Carl accepted the banker's hand and with his powerful grip, he crushed the banker's hand.

The banker withered in pain.

Carl spoke, "You can call me Carl now that we're business partners, C.C., and you know I'll shoot you down like a dog if you don't follow through with your part of the deal, don't you?"

"Yes, Mr. Butcher, I mean Carl!"

Carl released C.C.'s hand and placed a boot in his ass. Carl ended the business meeting.

"I'll be in communication with you through Mizel, part-ner, now get your ass back to the city." Carl laughed and fired three shots in the air. The terrified banker half stumbled, and half ran down the gravel road toward his black Cadillac.

THE BURNING

The Wild Cat went down easy. Bully sat, huddled in a fetal position, on the muddy ditch bank, anchored by thousands of willow trees in every conceivable shape and size. Through a wintery haze, he overlooked an ocean of cotton in the final stages of harvest. A light drizzle settled in and a distinct chill hung in the wet air. The muddy earth didn't matter. His clothes didn't matter. They were saturated with blood and mud after having butchered Miss Lillian's hog, earlier in the afternoon. The cold didn't matter; he kept warm with Wild Cat. Early winter brought the relentless rain and cold. The rain brought the mud, and the cold weather brought hog killing. God created Wild Cat whiskey for those who were subjected to mud and hog killing. Mud exhausted the flesh and hog killing destroyed the spirit. Bully allowed the whiskey to bathe his tongue, sooth his mouth, and send waves of warmth through his body. His thoughts turned to Willard. Tears made their way down his face. A sea of distorted cotton fields became a backdrop for the salty pain of his despair.

For Bully, Wild Cat presented an enigma. He sought the

numbing effects, yet the clear liquid loosened the gates to his wounded heart. Abandonment would have been the word to describe such a wound. Bully and the other souls between Eculatubba and Jug Fork didn't have such a word available to them. All they had was Wild Cat and Jesus. That terrible feeling didn't need the trappings of a word to bang at the gate. Rev. Strawrack would have screamed "There's power in the Word!" but the power behind the gates of Bully's heart would steamroll through a million words like a sickle of death through a field of lambs. Mr. John's love and affection placated the beasts for a length of time. After Mr. John's death, Bully's desperate attempt to seek the solace of Willard's company---an offering to the beasts---only infuriated the demons. Bully's last line of defense became Wild Cat whiskey and its numbing effects.

Bully emptied the last drop from the quart jar; a warm glow heated the gale force winds of his heart's anger and despair. A kind word from Mr. John or Willard would have provided Bully shelter, yet no word came, only the relentless building of warmth to fire, fire to fury, and fury to maelstrom. No rain, no word, no act of kindness quieted the rage once the demons escaped.

———

Bootleggers are night animals; they must be. Hard working folks, from town and country alike, toil by day: working in the fields; keeping the roads up; hauling milk; ginning cotton; and running the stores and shops. Come night fall, with aching backs, sore feet and the thought of having to get up and do it again—well, it's just too much for some folks, if they don't have whiskey. Besides, no self-respecting God fearing individual, black or white, man or woman, south of the Mason Dixon would risk being seen by the preacher or their neighbor buying whiskey. Southern folks buy their whiskey in the dark. That's where Carl came in. Like his daddy, Carl ran his bootlegging kingdom from sundown to first light.

"You boys git them bottles washed 'n filled." Mizel was in a good mood. Business had been brisk.

"The boss wants to see ya. Says he's got a little job," he said, raising his eyebrows.

As was customary, on a busy night, Carl broke out a jar of good whiskey after the last pickup drove off, around three o'clock in the morning.

"Boss says we peddled sum serous 'shine on dis night." Mizel screwed the lid off a Mason jar of Carl's finest. Mizel never touched the stuff himself. While the boys passed the jar of fire around, Mizel exhorted them to finish their task, Carl appeared from his office.

"I need six men who would like a little excitement tonight." Carl stared off into the distance. He talked to the lone light bulb in the room.

"Six men who want to endear themselves to me. Men who want to show ole Carl they are afraid of no man, except me, of course." Carl gave a little chuckle, turned his piercing eyes toward the mesmerized group and winked at his boys.

"What you got in mind, Mr. Carl?" a gangly blonde headed kid by the name of Fletcher broke the spell.

"A burning, son. A burning!" Carl's eyes flashed when a sense of excitement rippled through the room. Voices rose and movement became more animated.

"Hell, Mr. Carl, count me in," Fletcher responded along with the echo of several others.

"That's what I admire about most of you boys; you're ambitious and a little deranged, like me." Carl's gold fang sparkled.

"Mizel, put together your most eager five boys and meet me down at the shed in a half hour."

———

"I know this is hurting you, but you're gonna die if I can't get your calf turned 'round." Curtis ran his arm up to his shoulder inside the young heifer, again and again. She lay prostrate on the barn floor, eyes rolled back in her head, with subdued moans, each growing weaker from the eight hours of labor.

"Mr. John, I hope I'm doing this right," Curtis muttered to the heavens.

"There's a foot, I can feel it." He spoke to a chorus of four dogs and twelve cats who had made their home with Curtis.

"If I can just get my hand on his head," Curtis strained, "maybe I can turn 'um."

Sweat poured off Curtis. The wind howled through the barn timbers. He searched and probed. The dogs stationed themselves in a quiet vigil. The cats demonstrated a measure of concern, betraying their customary aloofness. The kerosene flame emitted long shadows. They danced across the massive timbers, bales of hay and long lines of stalls, which housed hundreds of mules, cattle and hogs.

———

Mizel's faded red truck cut through the darkness with the smell of gasoline, Wild Cat whiskey and taunting yells trailing away in the crisp fall night. Fletcher squeezed in between Mizel and Junior up front, straddling two five gallon cans of gasoline and three sawed off shotguns. Three of Carl's boys stood over the truck cab, screaming obscenities, passing whiskey around and throwing RC bottles at every road sign that came into view.

"You boys are in some kind of fine form tonight." Mizel grinned with an unlit cigarette in his mouth and a match in his hand.

"This is my first burning, Mizel! I've heard 'bout'um from some of the fellas but never thought I'd be asked to come along," Fletcher spoke, wild eyed with fear. He locked onto the match in Mizel's hand, amid the suffocating fumes of the gasoline.

"You boys jest do what Junior and me tell ya, and we might bring you again." Mizel raked the match across the dash of the old truck.

"Augh!" Fletcher screamed.

Junior's thick arm grabbed the terrified boy around the head.

"Damn, boy, will you settle down!"

The cold match fell between the two gasoline cans and Mizel regained control of the swerving truck.

"You need to git a grip on yourself, Fletcher. You gonna git us all killed." Junior spoke in a monotone voice amid the yelling and catcalls from the back of the truck. Junior released him and handed Mizel another match.

"They don't make 'um like they used to, Junior." Mizel laughed as the old truck headed for Ms. Lillian's place.

———

"There it is. I knew if it had a foot, it must have a head." Curtis spoke to no dog in particular. A young pup came up and starting licking Curtis in the face.

"Tippy, now you knock it off. Can't you see this is serious business? I ain't got no time to be messing with you."

The pup returned to his station. Curtis turned the calf's head. Contractions erupted and the heifer made chilling moaning and groaning sounds. The dogs barked and the cats headed for cover.

Curtis let out a howl. Blood, juice, slime, calf and after birth exploded in an antediluvian flood of new life. Curtis pulled the struggling newborn toward him and wiped the slime from its nostrils and eyes with his shirt tail. The calf struggled to get up from the barn floor. Possessed, the young mother struggled to her feet. Weak and exhausted, she lurched and fought to get her legs under her in much the same manner as her new calf.

"Easy! Easy!" Curtis comforted.

The new mother gained her balance and approached her new creation with trembling curiosity and concern. She licked, nuzzled and smelled the wet black and white calf. The calf made its instinctual search for the nectar of its mother's milk.

Curtis and his supporting cast of mutts and returning cats moved aside and watched in awe. The young mother and calf participated in the ritual of connection; old as the ages, yet extraordinary for the young mother and her calf.

———

Mizel cut the engine and lights. He crested the last hill before the long slow decline toward Ms. Lillian's barn. Junior banged on the back glass, signaling to the young bucks to become silent. The old truck coasted down the graveled road toward their destination. The full moon cast a faint light across the bottom. The huge timbered structure appeared, cathedral like, out of the darkness. Mizel turned the truck into an abandoned logging road and decided to traverse the remaining distance on foot. Amid faint whispers, creaks from rusty door hinges, and a log chain escaping from the truck when Fletcher tripped in terror, Carl's boys dismounted and loaded themselves with gasoline and shotguns.

"Boy, you make one more stupid move like that and I'll twist your head off and leave you out here for the buzzards." Junior said, yanking Fletcher back up to his feet.

"Your gonna wake up the whole damn county. Now, put that chain back in the truck and don't make a sound." Junior exclaimed. His hot whiskey breath faded; he pushed Fletcher to the ground. When Fletcher struggled to get the massive chain back into the truck, one of Carl's boys, slightly older, came over and assisted.

"Let's go. Let's get this over with."

Mizel led them off with a double barred sawed off shotgun over his shoulder. A shotgun toting Junior and the four young boys, who were taking turns carrying the cans of gasoline followed. Fletcher's can kept sloshing gasoline. He tripped and stumbled to keep up with the troupe.

The barn cast a long shadow across an expanse of land, crisscrossed with corrals and fences made from rough cut timbers. Muffled sounds of sleeping animals blended with the smell of honeysuckle and gasoline.

"Junior, you take Fletcher and pour gas down the sides of the barn, and then git back on up here; we'll cover you," Mizel said.

Junior motioned to Fletcher and they moved out. Junior poured gasoline while Fletcher struggled ahead under the weight of his can.

"What the hell are you doing, son?"

Junior's muffled voice chastised Fletcher. The boy labored to move the can further down the side of the barn.

"I stepped in a hog wallow," Fletcher whispered.

"Well, just git to it," Junior threatened.

With much effort, Fletcher splashed the gasoline along the oak siding and returned to Junior, reeking with its noxious smell.

"Boy, you gonna ride in the back of the truck going home," Junior said.

Junior and Fletcher joined Mizel and the others at the point closest to the truck. Mizel removed a Big Chief kitchen match from his bib overall's pocket and flicked the phosphorus head upon his hardened thumbnail. A yellow and blue flame burst from its head, illuminating Mizel's cupped hands and the faces of Carl's crew.

"Roast pig, boys?"

Mizel tossed the match toward the side of the barn. The howling wind overcame the flame until it fell into the gasoline drenched grass near the barn. Bright orange, red and blue flames exploded down its sides, leaping to the rafters. Heat poured from the flames. Vines erupted with loud, crackling sounds. Fletcher, gasoline drenched from the ordeal, burst into a human torch. The smell of hair and burning flesh pervaded the small group. He started to run across the barn lot. He screamed with his clothing a mass of flames.

"Kill him, Junior. Shoot him," Mizel ordered.

Junior raised the shotgun and for a moment, time stopped.

The troupe waited for the merciful blast.

"I-I just can't shoot him, Mizel." Junior lowered his shotgun.

Mizel grabbed Junior's shotgun and fired two rounds of double aught buckshot into the hapless boy. He fell over a fence, engulfed in flames. The barn exploded in a synchronous cacophony of waking animal sounds when the shots rang out. Mizel and his men ran for the truck, leaving Fletcher's charred body draped over a fence.

"Goddamn, Mizel! Why did you have to kill him?" The young man who had helped Fletcher with the log chain screamed. Tears streamed down his face.

"He was dead already, son. He just didn't know it. Get in the truck and shut up!" Mizel said.

Mizel started the truck and backed out on to the gravel road. Mizel looked over his shoulder to see the wind whipping the flames skyward. The burning barn lit the Mississippi landscape.

"I just couldn't pull the trigger, Mizel. I just couldn't make myself shoot that boy."

"Don't fret yourself, Junior."

Silence pervaded the truck cab. The whine of the transmission provided the only relief. Mizel knew he would never trust Junior again. Junior knew it, too.

Carl's boys were more subdued on the way back to Guntown.

———

Curtis drifted into a sweet sleep when he heard the gunshots. He jumped to his feet, slipped on his rubber boots and emerged from the tack room. Curtis's whole world was ablaze. Terrified horses, hogs and cattle joined in a chorus of death. Dogs barked, flames leaped, and the wind howled.

"Got to git them gates open. Mr. John would want me to get them gates open," he said, trying to reassure himself.

"Tippy, get outta this barn!" Curtis screamed.

Down the long hall, Curtis moved with great diligence: gate after gate... gate after gate... gate... gate after gate... gate after gate... the chains grew hotter and hotter... gate after gate... gate after gate... gate after gate... they opened... heat... terrible heat... running, animals running... stampeding... gate after gate... gate. after gate...

"Git! Git outta this barn... Got to get that baby calf."

Curtis scooped the young calf off the floor and ran toward the opening. Terrible animal sounds, dying animal sounds, falling timbers sounds, and windswept flame sounds roared from either side of the hallway. The wild-eyed mother ran after Curtis, head down, bellowing. Without warning, a giant support timber came crashing down, crushing Curtis's legs and trapping him under its tremendous weight. The newborn calf flew across the barn floor and the mother halted her run.

"Augh! Augh! Go, mamma! Take your calf and run!" Curtis's strained and pleading commands fell on the disoriented and stationary ears of the young heifer.

Mirage like, Bully appeared through the smoke and flames. Curtis's eye grew large when he realized Bully's presence.

"Bully get that calf and run for the corral. That way, the mamma will follow ya!" Curtis ordered.

"The hell with that calf, Curtis. I'm getting you outta here first!"

When Bully reached to help free him, Curtis hit and blocked his efforts.

"You ain't touching me till you get that baby calf outta here, Bully, and I mean it. Remember, Ms. Lillian said you got to do what I say, and I say get that baby calf outta this barn, Bully! Now!"

Exasperated, Bully lifted the calf, cradled it in his arms and began running for the giant opening. The bellowing mother followed in a staggering trot. While Bully ran, scared sober by the terrifying fire, amid the heat and sounds of anguish, the long hallway collapsed, spilling burning hay from the loft. Cascading waves of fire rained down. Bully heard Curtis' screams over the roar. Bully felt the terrible heat on his back. He hesitated. He turned to see the entire structure collapse around Curtis. Bully screamed in a dreadful anguish, born from the pain of the withering fire and from his utter helplessness. He resumed his reluctant exit from the barn and emerged, gasping for air, staggering and suffocating from the smoke and heat.

He placed the calf out of danger and returned to the opening of the barn. A wall of fire fed by the oak and hay greeted him with a searing heat; impossible heat.

"Curtis!" Bully screamed.

A huge draft horse appeared from the fire; wild eyed; flesh burning. It fell dead at Bully's feet.

The heat pushed Bully farther away. It was done. There was nothing left to do but watch along with the animals who had been lucky enough to escape. Bully slid to the ground, his back against a fence, and sobbed, gut wrenching sobs—sobs of loss, sobs of anger. and sobs of despair. Tears streamed down, streaking the soot and grime on his face. He clutched his stomach. Curtis's screams continued to ring in his head, over the horrible dying sounds of the trapped animals. Bully placed his hands over his ears.

JESSIE'S WORLD

You can't see 'um, but you can hear 'um, eyes popping outta your head, trying to see 'um. Nothing. Just fog. Thick fog. Soupy like fog. Buzzing. Voices, buzzing. Shuffling. Blue coats, shuffling. Moving. Marching. Heart in your throat. Ears pounding. The earth still covered with frost. Freezing. Creole boys talking funny. Giggling. Lips quivering. Bacon. The smell of bacon and gun powder.

"Mon Capitain! Mon Capitain! It's Mon Capitain!"

I turned my head to see the most magnificent figure astride a lathered, spirited black charger. It had to be the gallant Major John Pelham. The Creole gunner boys ran to him: excited and ready. I had heard about him and even talked to that Dalton fellah about him. But I'd never seen him. My first thought was---I would be willing to die for that man; strange; scary; but, unmistakable. He was impeccably dressed; not fancy, but neat. He had a beautiful red cloth around his hat, rich looking. My first thought was pretty. But men can't be pretty, can they? No, handsome. But, not in a hard way. A boy man. That's it. He was a boy man.

For a moment, I forgot the freezing.

The guns are ready. The men are ready. All waiting on the fog to lift. It is already happening. Very slow. Major Pelham loves his boys. You could tell by the way he smiles, jokes with them, even hugs them.

He'd hug me too, if I wasn't so new. I'm gonna walk right up to him and tell 'um who I am, freezing or not.

"Sir, Pvt. John Starke, sir. At your service."

"Where did you come from, son?" "Mississippi, sir!"

"How old are you, young man?"

"Almost thirteen, sir!"

"Can you swab a cannon?"

I thought I would die when he asked me that question.

"Yes, sir!"

"Report to the Sergeant on the Napoleon!"

"Yes, sir!"

I saluted the best I could. He mounted his black charger with the grace of a dancer and rode toward the Napoleon at a full gallop. The sun's presence burned the fog away.

The crusty sergeant is busy readying his gun and positioning his men when I walk up. The crew is not much older than me. Boys. They say they're from Louisiana and call themselves the Napoleon Detachment. The sergeant again asked me Major Pelham's question.

"Can you swab a cannon, Private?"

"With the best of them, Sergeant!"

Again, I lied.

"Got a name?"

"Starke, Sergeant. Private John Starke."

"Jean, take Starke here and use him as a reserve sponger."

"Me can do!"

Jean grabs my arm and pulls me toward this cannon. It's the biggest gun I've ever seen. When we get well beyond the Sergeant, I ask Jean the question that is exploding in my head.

"Jean, what's a sponger?"

"Mon Starke, zee sponger cool zee gun and put out zee sparks after she go boom."

A feeling of comfort came over me with that information. Jean introduces me to two of his fellow "spongers" by the names of Dominic and Paoli. They didn't look like any Confederate cannoneers my imagination had ever conjured up. Their uniforms consisted of anything they could find. If they once had uniforms, they were long gone. They're wearing shirts too big for them, boots stolen from dead Yankees and ridiculous coats in every size and description. Excitement and anticipation fill the cannoneers. I watch Major Pelham, erect in his saddle, giving instructions to his men on the Napoleon cannon.

BERTHA

Bully heard voices approaching. He moved away. He was in no mood to deal with Ms. Lillian, with field hands or with curious neighbors. He slipped to the west side of the burning barn and headed home to Alice Fae. Climbing over the third lot fence, he found the charred body of Fletcher, draped lifeless over a pool of blood.

Bully's mind raced. *Maybe Curtis wasn't stupid enough to destroy himself and burn his beloved barn down. Maybe this character, whoever he was, had something to do with it.* Bully moved in closer. Aided by the enormous light emanating from the burning structure, Bully saw the unmistakable telltale mark. The corpse bore a gold canine tooth, like Willard's. Carl made all his boys wear a golden left canine. Of course, Carl wore his on the right.

Bully forgot about home, Alice Fae and Jessie. His thoughts turned to Mr. John, Willard, and Curtis. He also thought about killing Carl Butcher. Black rage filled his heart. Thoughts of killing Carl Butcher flooded his mind and consuming him.

He thought of Mr. John's prized possession. He ran along the fence, jumped a small ditch, and hurled himself over a four-strand barbed wire fence. Limbs brushed his face and his heart pounded. Bully's long strides carried him along a worn path through the woods with one purpose: to reach the equipment shed. There, under a heavy chained door sat Bertha, Mr. John's special project. It had been off limits since his death. Bully crawled through a window. His heart raced. Mr. John's red monstrous creation sat in the shadows. Two winters and many rain-filled days were spent building Mr. John's dream: the most outrageous. huge mechanical beast his mind could conceive. Bertha was powered by two massive Caterpillar bulldozer engines with mammoth oversized tires in tandem. Four immense exhaust pipes protruded from the fine crafted metal work. Huge lights graced this behemoth. They could illuminate an area large enough for an all-night rodeo. To compliment her titan presence, Mr. John rigged a massive eight-foot-wide iron structure across the front: half cowcatcher and half battering ram. On the outer edges were staff like iron rods that protruded an extra six feet skyward. Bertha had no equal.

Bully prayed not for guidance, but for ignition—that the small auxiliary engine used to fire the larger engines would start. He grabbed the shotgun that kept by the door for intruding foxes, and with the assistance of a small lantern that hung on a nail by the door, Bully climbed toward the operator's platform. He used the deep cleats of the rear tires for footsteps. He secured the shotgun and stepped out onto the walkway with the lantern. He moved toward the auxiliary engine.

Gas. Yes. Choke. Okay. Bully turned the ignition and hit the starter. *Nothing. Dead battery. Damn.*

He grabbed the backup pull rope and secured the knot at

the end of the rope in the notched pulley on the crank shaft. Wrapping the rope with great care, he gave a mighty pull. Nothing. Again. Wrap. Pull. Nothing. Again. Wrap. Bully pulled with all his strength. The engine fired but died.

Again.

Wrap. Pull. The small engine sputtered and came to life. Bully feathered the throttle, adjusted the choke and nursed the engine until it ran at full throttle. He adjusted the throttle on the powerful main engines and pulled the lever connecting the auxiliary engine to the first engine. With the roar of a thousand lions, the engine fired. The earth shook. The tin roof rattled. Bully repeated the process, and again, the second monstrous engine came to life.

Bully hit the light switch and the entire shed area flashed with a blinding light. Squinting, his eyes adjusted. Bully depressed the powerful clutch and engaged the transmission. He released the pedal. The massive engines engaged the transmission. The tires moved. The machine lurched forward. Bully's hand pulled the throttle and the battering ram pierced the large wooden doors. They exploded with a thunderous crack over the roar of the engines.

The cold night air brought Bully to a higher state of alertness. His heart raced and his spirit soared, feeding off the smell of diesel exhaust and his decision to kill Carl Butcher. He moved down the lane and out onto the open road toward Guntown and Carl's place. When Bully passed the burning barn, he saw Ms. Lillian standing among thirty to forty neighbors, shaking her fist in his direction.

GALLANT JOHN PELHAM

There is really no way to describe the incredible sight the rising fog reveals. Miles and miles of Yankees, 125,000 strong, colorful banners flying, almost parade like, stretching up the Rappahannock River clear to Fredericksburg. Campfires and tents dotting the hillsides and the sun glistening off their cannons. The sergeant says our job is to prevent Gen. Franklin's men, all 55,000 of them, from moving in on Gen. Stonewall's right flank, whatever a flank is. All I want is to shoot that cannon and ride with Pelham, I mean Major Pelham.

Major Pelham is riding toward our position in a majestic gallop with his hat high in the air. He whirls around, rises in his stirrups and gives the command we all want to hear with a voice that echoes across the valley.

"Fire!"

My mind is blank for a split second; the cannon is so loud. The blue snake like movement of the Yankees halts, disoriented, no more than 500 yards from the Sarge, Jean, me and the rest of the Napoleon Detachment. Major Pelham is barking orders to us.

"Swab!" *Jean jumps forward and rams this wet mop on a stick down into the end of the Napoleon. I cannot believe how fast Jean moves. Jean is removing the swab the next command comes from Major Pelham.*

"Load!" *The Sarge and another cannoneer are loading powder and solid shot into the end of the cannon.*

"Ram!" *Dominic and Pialo move like lightning to secure the powder, shot and packing into the barrel.*

"Fire!" *Sarge ignites the cannon with thunderous effect.*

The Yankees fall to the ground: some dead and wounded; others just trying to survive. The giant blue snake stops, lurches backwards, then begins to move forward again.

"Swab!"

"Ram!"

"Load!"

"Fire!"

Each time Major Pelham barks his command, the cannoneers respond with deadly results. At once, I am envious, wanting to belong in the ranks of Pelham's men; to ride with Pelham. They rain down a terrible fire on those Yankees!

I know one thing with absolute certainty: it's more fun to shoot when the enemy is not shooting back. Fire, smoke and dirt begin to fly around our position. The rhythmic commands of Major Pelham become faint background music to the thunderous burst that falls around the valiant Napoleon Brigade.

"Limber up, men! Shift positions! Up the ridge, men! Move! Move!"

Pelham is magnificent. We hit. We move before the Yankees can find their range. I grab a swab and run behind the limbered-up cannon. A mule can run faster than you can imagine. The new position is even better. I can see across the valley toward the ocean of blue soldiers. Within minutes, the brigade is pouring shot after shot into the Yankees. With a fiery blast, a Yankee shell finds our position. Smoke, dirt, and shrapnel fill the air. Our cannon takes a direct hit, breaking the axel. Amid the confusion, Jean falls to the ground with blood gushing from his chest. Major Pelham is by his side.

"It hurts, mon Capitain," *Jean is saying.*

"You are a brave boy, Jean. I will get you to the surgeons as soon as we get the bleeding stopped."

Major Pelham comforts Jean like he is his own. Meanwhile, another Napoleon is doubling its fire. We move Jean away from the battle. Couriers are coming from Gen. Stewart, ordering and begging Major Pelham to retreat. He won't. He keeps declining until all the ammunition is gone. With nothing else to throw at the Yankees, except out hats, we retreat. What a glorious day!

Well, I'm not counting the Jean part.

HEADING TO CARL'S

Bertha sucked fuel through her oversized pistons. She begged for more. Fire poured from her great exhaust stacks. Bully's visions of Mr. John, Alice Fae, Jessie, Mamma, Willard and Curtis inflamed his rage for Carl Butcher. Mr. John would not stand for it! He would not be run off or burned out. Carl killed Willard. He killed Curtis; he would not stop. When Carl locked on his prey, he would not stop. Alice Fae, Jessie, or maybe Ms. Francina would be next. Carl always started with the weak then worked his way up. The high Sheriff Bigelow was worthless. No, Carl had to die tonight. Bully reached down and patted his shotgun. He felt his pockets stuffed with shotgun shells.

Mud Creek Bridge appeared in the distance. Approaching the structure, the fire in Bully's belly burned white hot with rage. He reached for the throttle and gave Bertha the last remaining bit of fuel. She surged. The huge tires struck the bridge's timbers. The structure shook. The monster rumbled toward Guntown.

JESSIE'S PROMISE

We're skedaddling back to Gen. Stuart's position with Jean, our cannons and equipment. Shot and shells fly from all directions. We take refuge in this old shack of a house and place Jean in an old iron bed. Jean ain't looking so good. His skin is ashen in color and he is drifting in and out of consciousness.

"Starke, can you shoot a musket?" Major Pelham asks.

"Yes, sir!"

"I am going to leave your here to take care of Jean as best you can. I'll send an ambulance wagon. You will not let me down, will you Starke?"

"No, sir!"

He gives me the prettiest musket you have ever seen and an ammo belt. I watch Major Pelham mount his horse and move his men out. I feel my chest about to burst with a warm feeling. I'll kill the whole Yankee army before I let Major Pelham down.

CARL MEETS BERTHA

"Mizel, you boys need to wipe that frown off your face and pay a bit more attention to the game. Otherwise, ole Carl is going to win what little money you got left."

Carl grinned. His hand revealed a pair of aces and a pair of deuces. Carl sent the rest of the crew home and waited for Mizel and the boys to return from their little chore. The loss of Fletcher upset the boys and Carl attempted to resurrect their spirit.

"You don't need to fret yourself over that Fletcher boy. It was his time and that is all there is to it. When it's your time, it's your time."

"I shouldn't have let him go, Mr. Carl." Mizel spoke. "He was willing, but he wasn't ready for burnings and such. He still was too much of a kid."

He forced himself to look through his cards.

"How else are you going to become a man, Mizel, if you don't get out there with 'um. That Fletcher boy was willing to venture out, I have to hand it to him. I'll take a card and make it a good one, Junior."

Carl threw an eight of clubs down and looked for an ace or a deuce.

"You must be pretty happy with that hand of yours, Boss. Just need one card, huh?" Mizel grinned.

"Maybe I am, maybe I'm bluffing." Carl spoke, stone faced. He stared at his cards.

"Do you hear something?" one of Carl's boys spoke up.

"The sound of your money moving from your pocket to my pocket, son." Carl laughed.

"No, I mean from outside."

"Yea, I hear something, too," Junior said.

"You boys just don't want to face the music concerning this fine hand of cards in my possession. It's probably a train."

A box of grits fell off a shelf and the single light bulb swayed from the ceiling.

Junior jumped from his seat and ran toward a window.

"That's no train I've ever heard!"

He never made it. Bertha's giant ram crashed through the wall impaling Junior. Bully unleashed an unforgettable Rebel Yell. The mighty blow knocked the entire building off its block foundation. Money, poker chips, bags of dog food and blood flew in all directions. The old potbellied heater crashed into the back wall. Carl, Mizel and the boys were knocked from their chairs by the impact and blinded by the bright lights when Bully illuminated the massive array of lights. Mizel gained his composure, rose to his feet and made his way toward his shotgun, which lay on the floor. Carl cursed and fired. His shots landed in the general direction of Bertha. Mizel reached for his shotgun. A twelve-gauge blast erupted from the wall of light, audible over the roar of Bertha's engines. Both barrels of Bully's shotgun hit Mizel in the gut, cutting Carl's most loyal boy in half. The impact knocked Mizel through a window and he fell dead on the ground outside the building. The two young men saw their chance and exited through a window. Bully throttled down Bertha, reloaded and jumped to the ground and landed in the store's rubble.

"Carl! Carl! It's me, Bully!"

The eerie sound of Bertha's engines, the long dark shadows, the crooked rows of shelving and the settling dust cast a surreal ambiance throughout the destroyed store.

"Thought you might like to meet Bertha!"

"That's the damnedest entrance I have ever witnessed, son!"

Carl's voice emerged from the darkness. Bully fired a shot in Carl's direction.

"Damn, son! We need to talk this out!"

Bully fired. Bang! He unbreeched his shotgun and reloaded. A hail of pistol fire erupted from the darkness.

"Augh!" Bully grimaced.

Blood seeped through Bully's pant leg. He fell to the floor. He returned the gunfire in the direction of Carl. Pain shot through his lower extremities. When Bully breached his shotgun to reload, the unmistakable sound of Bertha's engines roared to life and she lurched forward. *Carl had captured Bertha!* Bully rolled to the side. Bertha's mighty tires crushed chairs and tables and crashed through the back wall of the store under a hail of gunfire. Carl's maniacal laughter erupted.

Carl and Bertha emerged from the store's rubble, made a wide circle in the field behind the store and halted facing the wreckage. Carl reloaded his pistol, lit a cigar and with a deafening roar of Bertha's engines, rumbled forward. Bully fought to stay alert despite the pain of his wound. Bully caught a glimpse of Carl's sinister grin. The morning light broke over the trees. He crawled to a broken window and with much effort, placed his shotgun on the sill. Bully felt the ground shake. He cocked both barrels of his shotgun. *Had he reloaded in the confusion? Could he get a shot through the mass of iron and steel before him?* Bully's mind raced.

Bully felt his heart beating in his ears and sweat dripped from his nose onto the barrel. He aimed his shotgun between the massive exhaust pipes of Bertha. *Not yet... Not yet...* Junior's limp body still hung from the massive iron ram. Berth's giant tires threw dirt high into the air. Fire poured from the cherry red stacks. Death emanated from Carl's eyes. *Not yet... Not yet...*

Now! Bully squeezed both triggers. The shotgun fired. Bertha crashed into the building once again. Bully rolled into the corner. The shotgun went flying from the impact. Bertha knocked the last support from the building. The roof crashed down around him. He scrambled for his shotgun. Bertha exited the other side of the building. With much effort, Bully reloaded and waited for the next assault: it never came. An eerie silence prevailed. Bully, with much effort, got to his feet and with great caution, emerged from the devastation. He made his way past Mizel's body and limped toward what used to be the front of Carl's place. There sat Bertha across the road from the store as if waiting for Bully. He approached: shotgun cocked; and adrenalin flowing. There Carl lay, his crumpled body between the clutch pedals and gear shift: a lone buck shot wound between his eyes. His cigar clenched between his teeth with his grin intact. His body had crashed onto the kill switch; if it hadn't, Bertha would have been in Tishomingo county by now.

Bully felt exhausted. He wanted to go home to Alice Fae and Jessie. He wanted to sleep in his bed. But there were a few last things left to do. He hobbled back around the corner of the leaning store, and with considerable effort, he removed the long blue coat Mizel wore. It had been Willard's coat.

Bully put his ole friend's coat on and, with much effort, pulled Junior's dangling body from Bertha's ram. He climbed atop Bertha, took Carl's last cigar and threw Carl's limp body over the side. He touched the starter to the auxiliary motor. It came to life. Bully engaged Bertha's main engines and they roared to life. Bully turned toward home.

The sun peaked over the horizon. Bully made his way through Guntown and out onto the open road. His leg throbbed and ached, but it was only a flesh wound. While exhausted, Bully felt wonderful. For the first time in his life, he breathed air without living in Mr. John's shadow. He was his own man. *Maybe he would take Jessie and Alice Fae to the Delta and become a farm manager on one of those river plantations. He once had an offer to learn the sawmill business. Maybe he would look that fellah up again. Maybe Ms. Lillian would come to her senses and give him a chance to prove himself.* He lit Carl's cigar and inhaled. Exhaling the fine smoke from the cigar, Bully grinned. This was true freedom.

PROTECTING JEAN

While I watch over Jean, the battle rages outside. I can see the whole thing from a window overlooking the battlefield. I run back and forth, checking on Jean and watching the battle. Cannon balls are whizzing overhead, and men are yelling; dying. My musket is ready and I'm anxious to kill a Yankee. I know I could if I had a chance. Jean's sleeping and there is not a lot for me to do but pace back and forth and be ready to protect him.

TWO WORLDS COLLIDE

Bully pulled into the "mansion's" yard. The sun peaked over the willow trees behind the house. Alice Fae appeared through the front door on her way to Ms. Lillian's.

"Miss Lillian's gonna kill you, Bully, for getting Mr. John's contraption outta the shed! Where have you been?!" she shouted over the idling engines in disbelief.

"Taking care of a little business, darling. I've been shot. Come help me off Miss Bertha." Bully flicked the ashes from his cigar and hit the kill switch. Bertha shuddered. Her engines came to a stop.

"Shot!" Alice Fae ran around the huge tire and assisted Bully to the ground. "Where?"

"Guntown."

"Bully, don't play with me like that!"

"In the leg, that's all. I'm not going to die or anything. Just help me into the house."

"Bully, I been worried sick 'bout you!"

"Alice Fae, if I got to get shot every once in a while, to get some attention from you, it just might be worth it."

"Ms. Lillian is going to kill me for being late. I know she will."

Alice Fae helped Bully up the porch steps. Rover looked on. Struggling, they made their way up the rickety front steps and entered the front door. Jessie stood in the doorway of his bedroom with a musket in his hand, an ammo belt around his waist and a canteen around his neck. Jessie leveled the musket at Bully and Alice Fae.

"That is far enough, Yankees!"

"What the hell are you talking 'bout, Jessie!" Bully shouted.

"Put that gun down and help me to the bed."

"It's Pvt. John Starke to you, mister. My orders are to guard this position, and I'll kill you if I have to, soldier, wounded or not."

"Alice Fae, talk to him, I'm fading," Bully pleaded.

"Honey put the gun down and help your mamma. We got to get daddy to bed."

"My orders are to protect this house from Yankees, and I'll have to ask you to step away from that soldier, miss."

The young boy soldier cocked the musket.

"Jessie, are you crazy or something? Give me that damn gun!" Bully shouted and stepped toward the young soldier.

"Halt! Halt!" the young soldier shouted.

Bully limped forward; Alice Fae reached for Bully's belt. He grabbed the musket barrel. The young soldier fired. Alice Fae screamed. Bully fell to the floor, wounded in the chest. The young soldier began to reload, muttering under his breath.

"Swab, load, ram, fire! Swab, load, ram, fire."

The young soldier, satisfied he had killed his first Yankee, turned and left the room. His total concern was reconnecting with Major Pelham and his men. Bully died in Alice Fae's arms. She never made it to Miss Lillian's.

EPILOGUE

The Dogwoods are blooming, and folks still haven't quit talking about all the goings on down on the Watson place. One gossip wave after another splashed on these country folks, keeping everyone stirred up since Mr. John's demise down on Mud Creek. Harold Pepper and the rest of those old men over at the store put in overtime just to stay up with all the news. The crowning blow came when word got out that Doc Grasson and Judge Claxton met the day of Bully's killing. That meeting lasted most of the night. Doc convinced the judge that due to young Jessie's age and what had happened at that shack, no jury would convict him in a court of law. Those two old men also knew Jessie would wear a mark country folks would not forget. The confusing part for the judge, however, was this: *why was this old country doctor so interested in the boy?* Did Doc not have enough to do: patching up folks; tending his roses; and stomping over ever battlefield brought on by that Yankee invasion?

What Doc revealed had all the women folk leaving their quilting frames and reaching for the smelling salts. According to Doc, Mr. John had raped that woman back in his youth after a drunken night at the county fair; nine months later, Bully was born. The judge just took a deep breath and pushed himself away from the table. Doc told how he delivered the child and overheard the poor woman cursing Mr. John while in a morphine stupor. Doc kept his secret for all these years. After her family disowned her, Mr. John had some remorse for his dirty deed and attempted to do the right thing by the girl and child---not without a price, however.

When Doc and the judge emerged from their meeting, both agreed that Jessie would have to leave the county to have any semblance of a life. Doc agreed to speak with Alice Fae. She went along with Doc and the judge's views but balked at leaving herself. She squalled and cried, but in the end, she would not leave that farm and what she knew. Exasperated, Doc made a bold move and took it upon himself to get Jessie out of the county. They loaded that old Chevy with bags and dog: and left early one morning, some say toward New Orleans. The real shock came when Miss Francina met them with her bags packed and loaded in, too. Miss Lillian was heartbroken at the thought of her Francina leaving, some say. Alice Fae caught the worst of it, but the old woman recovered. Folks saw her buying cotton seed for the spring planting, and Judge Claxton gave her a talking to for taking that Oldsmobile and running C.C. Bates off the road one afternoon. Some say she grinned when she stepped off the porch, leaving the judge's office. Oh, yes, Beaufort King moved in and from all appearances, the Wild Cat never stopped flowing from those hills; that's hearsay, of course.

ABOUT THE AUTHOR

Kelly Ferguson is a Southern storyteller. The art of story-telling is a powerful tool: to engage; to communicate; and to create the magic of humor. Kelly Ferguson is a master. Whether on the written page, before a group, or in the healing arts Kelly Ferguson is a force. He is a husband, father, brother, healer and farmer in recovery.

Kelly Ferguson can be reached by email at:
kferguson@fairparkpublishing.com